Flea Market Weirdos

and

Other Stories

—

Anthony Abelaye

From 2005 to 2018, I wrote a zine called *Whuddafug*, which I later renamed to *Koogmo*. During this period, I published around twenty issues sporadically. There was no set schedule. Whenever I had enough material for a zine, I'd call it done and head to the local Staples or Office Depot to make the photocopies.

Each issue was anywhere from 20 to 25 pages in length, photocopied on 8.5x11-inch paper and stapled in the upper-lefthand corner. About as DIY and simplistic as you could get. I opted for speed and efficiency over traditional book publishing standards. A few readers commented that it looked too amateurish. My response was always: "This is by design."

It was way faster to get that copy machine to churn out fifty to a hundred copies at a time. All I had to do after that was fold each issue in half, crease the spine with something heavy like a paperweight, and off I went, leaving copies all over town – outside thrift shops, on coffee shop tables, in news racks outside grocery stores. Sometimes I'd stop by the Greyhound bus station in downtown Dallas and leave a few copies on one of the benches, weary and unwashed travelers watching me with bored curiosity.

Within the first year or two, I had gained a handful of subscribers, mostly from the U.S. and Canada. Although I had a few one-offs from other countries, like Australia or Singapore. My mainland subscribers would send me $1 each month through the mail, and I'd send them a copy of my latest issue as soon as it was ready. Maybe I could have charged more, but a dollar seemed a fair price.

But I noticed a disturbing trend. I began receiving more and more requests for copies of my zine from people doing time in U.S. prisons. Copies were always free to prisoners, and I guess word started getting around. Maybe they were trading my zine for cigarettes or sexual favors – I don't know.

Each month, I'd receive three or four letters from guys doing time in the big house. Often they would include sketches or handwritten stories of how they ended up in prison, detailing the crimes they committed (mostly drug-related), where their lives went wrong, who was to blame, etc. Some wrote to proclaim their innocence. One guy kept sending me foot fetish stories and included drawings of women's feet. Another would send letters written entirely in crayon and relate stories of his life in an almost child-like and whimsical demeanor, stringing each sentence together like a sing-songy nursery rhyme and drawing little hearts and happy faces in the margins.

This was my fault – not because these guys were in prison, but that they were sending me so much material. I had made the mistake of including a blurb at the end of each issue, requesting submissions from readers – stories, sketches, etc., and that's exactly what these guys were responding to. But it was too much stuff. Too much of the same depressing "How I ended up in prison" story over and over again. There were too many people in prison. Each time I opened my post office box and discovered yet another letter bearing a penitentiary return address, I felt annoyed, saddened, hopeless. We've become an incarceration nation. I don't know what the numbers are as far as total number of prisoners (I'm too lazy to Google it at the moment), but it must be in the millions. And each month, more and more were requesting copies of my zine.

I was growing weary of it. Instead of *Koogmo* becoming some underground zine classic, like Cometbus or Dishwasher Pete, I had become a pen-pal for prisoners.

It seemed that my DIY publishing and distribution efforts had backfired. This isn't what I had in mind when I set out to make my stories and essays freely available for people to read – I didn't mean only the people serving twenty-five to life for murder or dealing drugs. Although, thinking back on it now....I probably had more people reading my zine than some college literary mags. Not just by prison inmates, but by the dozens of copies I left out in the wild. But maybe laundromats and thrift shops weren't the best places to find fawning literary groupies.

It was time to refocus. Time to think bigger.

What you hold in your hands is a result of that effort. Ten years of short stories and essays.

Enjoy!

– anthony (aka "koogmo")
September 2022

You tire of your old haunts out there in the grimy, run-down Tenderloin district of San Francisco. Comes a night you decide to branch out, head out to the lower Haight. You've heard cool stories of cool things happening to cool people. Or strange things happening to weird hippies and teenage runaways. You go to investigate, stumbling out of a taxi somewhere near the vicinity of Steiner and Haight. Close enough. You wander to the nearest bar. Pubs, clubs, cafes -- they prefer to call them. Shadows standing around outside, milling about. Cool, hip shadows. Attitudes displayed like badges. White kids from Midwestern suburbs paying rent to Chinese landlords now. Nobody grows up in the Haight. Drug addicts come to die, homeless come to live, but nobody grows up in the Haight. Some giggling, some ego-assertive laughing, but mostly a lot of standing around. This is what you believe, but nobody gives a shit. You spend most nights in Tenderloin bars staring at toothless old men staring back at you and the hags there trying to hustle them at the bar and the Mexicans trying to hustle them at the pool table. The only differences between that crowd and this one are about twenty years and a mouthful of their own teeth.

You order a beer and then order four more. Out of money. Forgot to bring more. You'll be walking home tonight, and that's when you meet her. Cute chick. Hip. One of the shadows milling about outside. This one's by her lonesome a few doors down, smoking a cigarette. She's watching, observing, spying. Her name's Justine, she tells you. You exchange phone numbers. The next day she calls you from the psychiatric ward at San Francisco General. It's a collect call. Just wanted to talk, she says. Feeling optimistic, possibly lucky, you agree to meet her at her apartment the next day. Assuming her parents are willing to sign the hospital's required release forms.

You try to be understanding, compassionate, but you'd just met her the night before, and you're having some difficulty keeping up with her monotone monologue, something about things that occurred when she was a child. Like overhearing the bus stop conversations of a deranged old woman, you can't help but be drawn into it while simultaneously trying to keep your distance. You wonder what attracts these sorts of people to you -- perhaps some special power, a psychic beacon, some kind of animalistic attraction -- something that people pick up on and are somehow drawn toward. Or maybe the girl is just fucking crazy. And you -- you simply do not matter in her world. You are like the bug she squashes against an invisible wall.

You arrive at the address she'd given you over the phone. It's a place not far from your own hovel just up the street. You ring her at the buzzer. She tells you to take the elevator to the basement.

(Basement?)

You call bullshit. You sniff a setup, a con job. She's waiting to kill you -- with a knife, a hatchet, a brick and her bare hands. Only garbage and cockroaches live in basements. She's gonna fuckin' kill you, man. Get outta there now. She's gonna rob you, take your wallet and the sixty-some-odd dollars it contains. She'll dump your bloodied corpse into one of the trash bins. Then she's gonna take your driver's license and use it to forge a hundred others in an effort to bring her Honduran boyfriend across the border and all of his extended family and friends. It's a fuckin' scam, I'm telling you. Get outta there NOW.

But you brought a condom.

Just past the garbage cans and before the utility meters, a door is cracked open in the middle of the brick wall. She peeks out and sees you. Her look is one of non-recognition. There is no smile, no wave. Just a blank stare.

You smile and wave. She bids you in like a perfect stranger. Like you're arriving for a dental appointment.

Her little studio apartment isn't the gloomy and damp place you'd first imagined. There is no lone light bulb swinging on a chain in the middle of the room. The place is actually quite warm and sunny. Two large windows overlook a small garden out back.

Her father pays for the place, she tells you. She sits upright on the edge of her bed, straight and proper, one hand resting calmly on each knee. She doesn't look at you. She isn't looking at anything. She's just staring off into space, lonely little girl in her lonely little basement apartment.

You're standing off to the side in a somewhat defensive posture, waiting to be attacked.

Then you notice the ants. They're everywhere. They're not just marching single-file, staying nice and organized along the corners where the floor meets the wall. They're swarming all over the place, agitated and frenetic, real crazy like. All over the floor, all over the kitchen sink, the dishrack, covering the wall area near the light switch. Something has obviously angered them. Perhaps it was your arrival that set them off.

You've never been good with pets. Maybe it's the same with household vermin.

Oh, the ants, she says. She's having a slight problem with them. Unmindfully, she brushes a few off of her leg. You see them crawling all over and between the covers on her bed.

You remain standing. Not that there's anything to sit on -- except for her bed, the place is bereft of furniture or furnishings. Even the windows lack blinds or curtains.

I hope they're not the biting kind, you joke. She ignores you, and still looking straight ahead, continues her monologue where she'd left off the night before. She relates a series of events that occurred when she was a teenager, something about a best friend and a misinterpreted note that was left in one of their lockers. You've since lost track of whose locker it was or what the note was about. Her voice drones on and on, as if she is the disinterested narrator in a movie only she can see. You've been standing now for half an hour. Your legs start to tire. Your knees begin to buckle. You're not a horse, after all. Damning the ants, you take a seat on the bed next to her. You notice her breasts, firm and plump, perky, resting just beneath that thin layer of a flimsy thrift store t-shirt. Her nipples are outlined perfectly. Pink, you imagine. A delicate pink.

But the phone rings, and she jumps up to answer it.

Yes. Yes, she says. Come by later. I'll be home.

She hangs up and returns to her seat on the bed next to you. It was her father, she explains. He's coming by later to fix her door. It doesn't lock. A man came into her apartment the other night while she was getting ready for bed. A black man. She leaves it at that. You feel something crawling up your arm, and you brush it away.

She remains silent. You reach out and caress her soft shoulder-length hair. Slowly, gently, you pull her toward you. There is no resistance. You guide her down toward the mattress. She remains limp as you kiss the nape of her neck.

How much have you got?

Sixty.

Okay, she says.

As an unsuspecting parent with a school-aged child, you find yourself obligated to attend various school functions throughout the year. Insidious little invitations and announcements arrive in the form of little red, blue, or yellow flyers planted amongst the miscellaneous papers that your kid brings home. Christmas play, spring chorus, bake sale, book sale -- all that nonsense. For some reason, most of that stuff is scheduled AFTER school hours. After all, they do want to include the parents, so instead of coming home from work and vegetating out on the couch or in front of the computer, we've got to drag our tired asses out to the kid's school and engage in the lunacy that is part of the public education experience.

I don't remember having to deal with any such hassles when I was in elementary school. Back then, school faculty weren't as perky and hyperactive as they seem to be today, where the social aspects of schooling takes higher precedence over the basics of just learning to read and write. This practice evidently carries over into high school, where barely literate kids are allowed to graduate simply to get their dumb asses out of an already over-taxed system and into the very sad and real world of minimum wage jobs -- warehouse engineering, fastfood service technicians, retail sales analysts.

I realize I'm sounding like an old geezer when I say "Back in my day," but so be it. I'm an old geezer. In the eyes of my 7-year-old, I'm nothing more than "fat, squishy Daddy, squishy old man." But back in my days, when we were done learning those most basic of basics, the teachers would kick our asses out onto the playground where we were left to fend for ourselves. Nobody cared. Yard duty teachers were only there to lend an unsympathetic ear to the rats and the finks. As for the rest of us: To each his own. The purest form of Darwinism took over whenever that recess bell sounded. With regard to your own ass, it was kick or be kicked. Maybe it was different for girls or those less prone to violence in the schoolyard. In fact, I'm pretty sure it was. The girls and the future homosexuals stayed near the blacktop playing four-square and twirling on the monkey bars, while fist-fights and all-out war was waged between the boys out on the soccer/football field. Alliances were formed and enemies were made that would last years, or at least until we made it to junior high.

I can't say that I was an antisocial child (that state of mind came much later). I was simply disinterested in socializing. All that stuff seemed geared toward the female mentality, anyway -- the socializing, the decorating, the party planning, dressing up all pretty and clean, going out and being seen in the scene.

It all came full circle the other day when I got home from work. There on the kitchen table, resting atop Sara's homework folder was a bright red piece of paper, a Christmas invitation, an invitation to the lighting of the Christmas tree at Fremont Hub, a little outdoor, half-empty shopping mall just down the street.

Nadjet was getting ready for work. She recently got a part-time gig at the Hollywood Video down the street. "Can you take Sara tonight?" she says.

"Where?"

"To her Christmas function. It's tonight at Fremont Hub. I told you about it the other day, remember? I told Sara I was going to take her, but I forgot I had to work tonight."

"Oh." I turn to Sara, who's also getting ready. "Sara, are you sure you want to go? It might be too cold."

"Yes! Mommy can't take me, so YOU have to take me. All my classmates are going to be there!"

Damn.

We arrive a few minutes early. The festivities aren't scheduled to begin until six o'clock. The place is dark, literally, like someone forgot to switch on the lights when the sun went down. We could see shadows milling about in all the blackness, somewhat illuminated by the light leaking out of the few storefront windows.

"Are you sure there's something going on here tonight?" I say to Sara. "The place looks pretty empty."

"Yes!" she says. She's excited, eyes darting about, scanning, searching for her classmates.

Then we see a small gathering of shadows surrounding a much taller shadow, the Christmas tree that will presumably be lit up. Metal folding chairs have been placed in front of it a few rows deep. We join the quiet crowd. People are just sort of standing around, expectant. Sara is busy searching every short person to see if it's someone she recognizes.

"There's Timmy!" she yells, standing just five feet away and pointing at him. He and his mother look at us and smile.

"I see Kyle! Look! There's Ms. Magnani!"

"I don't know any of these people." I say.

"Of course you don't," says Sara. "You're not in my class."

Off to the side, I see a band setting up their equipment -- a saxophonist, keyboardist, and drummer. Seasoned musicians, I figure. Tall, thin black guys, old and weathered-looking, session cats

-- gonna be jamming to some Christmas tunes real soon, I think. These guys look like they really know how to play. The saxophonist taps on his microphone and addresses the crowd. He looks hungover and sounds as tired as he looks. Seems to have lived the blues more than played them. The band launches into an instrumental rendition of "Chestnuts Roasting Over An Open Fire". They're playing a few clicks too slow. The sax player and keyboardist aren't playing in the same key. It all sounds slightly off-kilter, kind of wobbly like the sax-playing band leader. I think, well hey, who else are you going to get to play for a half-hour on a Tuesday night in December?

The band starts playing "Jingle Bells." The band leader isn't really singing the song -- he's just sort of mumbling "Jingle bells...jingle bells...bum-bum-bum-bah-dum..." Then he pauses, the music comes to a hesitating stop, and he says into the mic, "Does anyone know the rest of the words?"

Huh? You hire a band to play Christmas songs, and they don't even know the words to "Jingle Bells?!" These guys must really need the money. And they really need to rehearse. I'm starting to think I could do better with my beat-up acoustic guitar and a kazoo. The band never fully recovers and they just kind of stop playing altogether.

A few moments later, a man steps up to the podium in front of the unlit Christmas tree. He says he's the director of something or other at Washington Hospital. A few people clap. Then he introduces the Mayor of Fremont.

"Look!" I whisper into Sara's ear. "It's the mayor of Fremont!"

"Really?" she says, looking around. "Where? Where?"

The mayor steps to the podium. He's a tall man, at least six-four, six-five. He is old and sleepy. They must have roused him from his nap at the retirement home. Hunched over, moving very slowly, deliberately like my grandpa -- every movement requires concentration and focused coordination between all body parts. He looks as if he's going to nod off right there at the podium. He says something about what a great city Fremont is and mumbles a few more words about Christmas and the unlit tree behind him before the director at Washington Hospital takes the mic and lets the mayor shuffle back to wherever he came from, probably bed.

"And now," says the director from Washington Hospital, "let's start the countdown."

5...4...3...2...1...click-click...there is a momentary pause where disappointment and failure begin to creep into everyone's minds. Then the lights go on. The crowd mumbles a flaccid "Yaayyy..." More a sigh of relief, really. Just plain white lights that aren't any fancier than tiny white light bulbs, about as impressive as watching a next-door neighbor switch on a porchlight. "The tree of life!" I yell. A few people turn to look at me. Nevermind.

Bell-ringers from one of the local high schools are scheduled to perform. They move into position in front of the tree as quickly as the darkness will allow (the dim lights on the tree aren't much help), fumbling and trying to stand in the correct order, low to high or is it high to low? The guy in the middle is safe. The ones on the ends need to switch.

They begin playing, but the bells are chiming too softly. We can barely hear them. They should have mic'ed each bell. Everyone sort of leans forward and inward, straining to listen. The crowd closes in around the bell-ringers, trying to figure out what song they're playing.

Someone must have notified mall employees about the insufficient lighting. Two maintenance workers drag construction floodlights out to the area, strung along what appears to be a mile's worth of bright orange extension cord. They set up directly behind the bell-ringers and aim the lights right at the crowd. When they switch them on, the intense beam of light temporarily blinds the people sitting in the first few rows. The silhouettes of the bell-ringers stretch out across the crowd. Now instead of being too dark, it's too bright. People have to shield their eyes.

The bell-ringers continue to play, but the crowd still can't hear what they're playing and soon loses interest. People start talking and chatting, which drowns out the chiming even further. Small kids start tripping and playing with the bright orange extension cord. The crowd is beginning to disperse. A few have wandered down to the Barnes & Noble bookstore. Others are heading over to Target.

I pull out my cell phone and check the time. Just past 6:30. "Ready to go?" I say to Sara.

"Yeah," she says. "It's getting boring."

"Let's go home, then."

"Okay."

A half-hour night out on the town. I hope this continues all throughout her teen years, but I somehow doubt that.

12

Friday I returned to the city and revisited my old neighborhood haunts from a decade ago, back when there was a skinnier man roaming those streets with a pack-a-day habit and a slight drinking problem. Will these streets remember my name? Will it be like old times, and everything old will seem new again, as when I first discovered them? Geographically, everything is the same. What else remains?

I stayed at the City Center Hostel on Ellis and Larkin, right along the rim of the heart of the Tenderloin. I'd argued with Nadjet earlier that morning because she had gone out the night before and didn't get in till two in the morning. Waited up for her, feeling jealous and insecure. I'm old enough to recognize now that the real problem lay within me and had nothing to do with Nadjet. It's as Edgar Cayce said, just as all the Buddhist teachings, just as Jesus had probably taught: All life is self meeting self. As I had done, so had it been done unto me. I was only getting my own, as the saying goes.

So when I got home from work Friday afternoon, I packed up my backpack, thinking that I'd stay in the city at least till Monday morning, but telling Nadjet that I'd be gone a week. I'm leaving eighty bucks in the can, I told her. Better make it stretch. I tried to appear aloof, detached, without a care and unmindful. I headed out the door without saying good-bye and hoofed it to the BART station. My goal was simple: Drink then walk off the drunkenness. I aimed to wander around just as I had been doing once a week for the last few weeks. Nothing special, just wander, meander, watch and observe. It's when I'm not expected to do or be anything that I feel most like myself.

The train got into town with rush-hour under way, but it didn't matter because I was going the opposite way. Most BART commuters live in the East Bay and points farther out -- Concord, Pleasanton, Walnut Creek. How many times had I ridden that train into the city? I never tire of the ride. The train is a silver ghost passing through the backyards of people's lives. We see the clutter, the mess -- old bicycles, scrap metal -- the ubiquitous blue tarp, tattered and torn, covering, hiding unknown humps and clumps -- old beat-up cars, old beat-up sheds, weeds, wildflowers growing in pleasantly unexpected places -- next to abandoned railroad tracks, along polluted ditches, and in once case, in rain gutters along the

13

roof of someone's house. Sometimes we'll catch glimpses of the people who live in these places, and it's like spying an animal in the wild. We see them operating in their natural habitat. Filthy white t-shirt with beer gut hanging out, smoking cigarettes, watering lawns that, from our vantage point on the elevated tracks, appear to be no more than hopeless postage stamp-sized patches of green awash in a sea of urban wasteland and urban decay, a sea of cracked concrete, rotting wood, torn up asphalt, bad roofing and weeds -- great wide expanses of gray, brown and rust, and then little bright patches of green dotted here or there. So pointless are these front lawns that dot the American landscape.

When the train reaches San Leandro station, we enter the industrial zone -- junk yards, roofing material companies, tube companies, scrap metal yards, recycling plants, and my favorite, the shipping container reseller and the Port of Oakland with all their shipping containers stacked four or five stories high, stacked up neatly and efficiently as only shipping containers and milk crates can be stacked. I hope to live in one of these some day, on a couple acres of land I plan to buy in the high desert of northern Nevada, but that's another story.

Passing overhead on these elevated tracks, we spy grungy blue-collar workers operating those tractors, those trucks -- it's all blue jeans and steel-toed boots out here. We see the homeless encampments, the trash-strewn belongings, the seeming haphazard lives that are lived and forgotten.

We see the old Mother's Cookies factory, the driving range, the U.S. postal service mail truck training ground, abandoned cars, abandoned school buses. Wait, looks like someone's living in that one. The sheets as curtains are tacked up along the windows, decorated just so, at home along the road in an abandoned part of town.

Passing overhead on these elevated tracks we look down upon the grime, the filth, the creeping blight, all things that encompass the ugliness, the vileness of modern life incarnated in the form of decrepit buildings and decrepit sidewalks, festering weeds and toxic puddles.

We glide overhead, looking down, superior, aloof, detached. Or so we like to think.

I ride the train as far as Civic Center station and hike up the stairs to the city streets. How many times have I traveled this route and in how many different frames of mind? I ponder the ghosts that surround me pondering the same thoughts. Do subways even have their own ghosts? Maybe in Japan. Everything is haunted there.

First thing was to find a place to crash for the night. I didn't want to look like a dork drinking in those Tenderloin bars while strapped to a backpack. I was already feeling vulnerable, why look like a target? Better to travel light.

I hiked up Hyde looking homeless and poor in my ratty surplus army jacket and came across a horde of Critical Mass bicyclists. On the last Friday of each month, they take over the streets and ride as one rag-tag mass from the Ferry Building downtown all the way out to Civic Center and Van Ness, blocking traffic, ignoring red lights, pissing off commuters stuck in their cars. It appeared to be a bunch of twenty-year-old kids with nothing better to do, many of whom probably left their cars discreetly at home that day. A once-a-month occurrence. Better to go your own way and think your own thoughts. Riding along and following this crowd is really no different than riding along and following any other crowd. What is protesting, anyway, but a benign form of terrorism, a bitching and moaning form of terrorism which tries to force an idea or set of ideas upon others? It's the minority whining about the majority until they themselves become the majority. Without the safety of the crowd exactly who are these individuals? That's what they should be asking themselves. It shouldn't matter where you stand as long as you stand strong in your own beliefs, beliefs that you yourself have come upon through your own efforts. Change always comes from within, when it is realized, and it's never about getting clobbered over the head with someone else's ideas of a perfect utopia. Do your own fucking thinking, man. Get on with your own fucking life. Stop following the crowd and start telling yourself what to do. Neo-hippies are no better than neo-conservatives. It's all a form of funky fucked-up conformism.

I walked up to what used to be the Astoria Hotel on Ellis and Larkin and discovered that they were now a part of Hostelling International or some such organization. The building itself was now called the City Center Hostel. Eighty-five bucks a night for a private room with no television, no phone, no stationary, no desk lamp, for that matter, by which I could get some writing done if I had wanted. The tiny wash basin of a sink was situated right over the toilet in such a way that you had to first bend into an L-shape and slide yourself under the sink if you wanted to take a seat on the crapper. But I didn't mind. The room itself was still bigger than my first apartment, which was an ascetic ten-by-twelve room with side appendages for a bathroom and a kitchenette. I lived in that little hole for seven years until it became overrun with cockroaches and cigarette smoke. The walls were stained a dark yellow from all the years of chain-smoking Marlboros with the old creaky window cracked just a little. I'd read stories about cockroaches finding their way into people's ears, and when I started finding little baby cockroaches in the empty beer bottles sitting atop the stove and finding them in my sheets and around my pillow, I knew it was time to get the hell out of there. At first, I considered sleeping in a coffin, but when I called a mortuary to get a quote, the guy on the other end of the phone explained that coffins weren't really made for sleeping in. I couldn't afford one at the time, anyway -- the price of a new coffin was a few hundred dollars more than a normal bed. I doubted I'd be able to find used ones. This was before eBay and craigslist, of course, where I would look now if I were interested in such things. I probably could've bought one from some recovering goth chick who had lost weight and was in the process of jettisoning the black makeup and black clothes.

—

Dinner was at the usual spot: Little Henry's on the corner of Post and Larkin. Hamburger sandwich well-done and a bottle of Miller Genuine Draft. I had always ordered the Parmesian porkchops or the spaghetti with meatballs (only two and no more), but not tonight. Everything is good there, as long as you don't mind the strung-out transvestites; the clammy-skinned perverts, eyes darting about for boy-whores; the confused old people who have been living in the neighborhood for too many years, stumbling through the door half-drunk and speaking a few decibels too loud, missing a few teeth, bad breath. If you can ignore all of that and stay focused on the good cheap food, you'll be okay and you will enjoy a fine dining experience. Cops eat there, too. Motorcycle cops, the guys driving the squad cars, detectives, vice squad. You can spot them easily and pick them out from the usual denizens, the ones who aren't wearing uniforms, I mean. They sit confidently and maintain a steady eye contact when they catch you looking at them. They're bigger and healthier looking than the usual slouches, resting securely in the power they know they wield over the general populace. And they all have mustaches. I don't hate them, but I don't trust them, either. They're San Francisco cops, and they can beat you down and leave you in a bloodied pulp on the sidewalk and get away with it, but when you see them gathered in one place eating on a regular basis, you can trust that place will be cheap and good.

—

If you're going to do any kind of drinking, you're going to need water. The more alcohol you drink during the night, the more water you'll need at the end of it. Something I learned a long time ago that has worked well for me over the years -- no matter how drunk I was when I came stumbling home after another bout of drinking and shooting pool, I always tried to drink as much water as I could before falling into bed. I'd shove my face under the bathroom faucet if I needed to. Downed as much of it as I could without spitting it back up. Try this, and you'll see. Come morning, all that water you drank will help ward off a bad, axe-in-the-head type hangover, not always but most of the time, and all you'll need to deal with are the dry hairy shits and the consequences of whatever the hell you may have done the night before while you were in that cozy drunken stupor.

—

So I'm down the street and around the corner in the little grocery store/market that sits between my favorite Goodwill store and the bar in which I plan to start my evening's festivities. These three places, my job, and my apartment were all I needed at one point in my life. You could have blown everything up, razed everything else in that entire stinking city, and I would have been just fine. Nowadays, I commute thirteen miles to my job. Our shopping is done at the Food Maxx five miles down the road. My world has expanded, unfortunately, in ways that I had always hoped to avoid.

I'm shopping for my water and a toothbrush and toothpaste. Then I start searching for the baby wipes because that's how I like to finish off after I've done my deed on the crapper -- toilet paper alone doesn't cut it for me anymore. Baby wipes do a better job of cleaning up the wet drips. But the place doesn't have any in stock, so it appears I'll be roughing it tonight. I glance up and see this guy at the end of the aisle staring at me sideways.

"Eric!" I say. My old pool-shooting partner, drinking buddy from eight, nine years ago. He and I in that bar on the corner every night, all night, Korean bar girls serving up the drinks, plunking those quarters down into the side of the pool table, game after game, night after night, two, three years straight. At the end of that run, I ended up owing the IRS fifteen grand from a tech job I'd been working, getting paid cash every week, most of it having been spent in that bar buying drinks and literally pissing it all down that barroom toilet.

My friend Eric could have passed for Eric Clapton, and now he looked like a slightly chubbier version. He said he didn't really drink anymore, wasn't really into that dive bar scene on account of getting punched in the teeth one night and getting his knee broken by some drug-addled maniacs who were in there hassling one of the bar girls. The cop who showed up some time later said it wasn't worth filing a police report since he probably wouldn't be able to find the guys who did it. So Eric was left hobbling around on crutches for a month or so, which sucks when you live alone, you're getting old, you have no car, and you still got to make it to work ten blocks down into the financial district. Shortly after, his company laid him off after eleven years of service. His severance package was one month's pay. Now he's learning to teach English as a second language and planning to move to Thailand.

We were in our bar now drinking a few rounds for old time's sake, reminiscing over things that hadn't really changed much to begin with. But drunks like to reminisce and so we were drunks once again. The jukebox was playing that same old tired song:
WHAT IS LOVE? BABY DON'T HURT ME...DON'T HURT ME...NO MORE...WHAT IS LOVE...?
Annoying. Painfully so with the volume turned up full blast. Eric and I were sitting across from each other one one of those bar tables that are barely large enough to hold a napkin and two drinks, and still we had to yell at the top of our lungs to hear each other.
"I DON'T RECOGNIZE ANY OF THESE PEOPLE!" I said.
"YEAH! DIFFERENT CROWD!"
"WHO ARE THOSE KOREAN GIRLS BEHIND THE COUNTER?"
"I DON'T KNOW! I DON'T REALLY COME HERE ANYMORE!"
"SAME OLD SONGS ON THE JUKEBOX!"
"HAH!"
"I HATE THIS FUCKING SONG!"
WHAT IS LOVE? BABY DON'T HURT ME...DON'T HURT ME...NO MORE...WHAT IS LOVE...?
It's true -- the more things change, the more they stay the same. It was the same crowd. I'd been gone for almost a decade. I return one night, and it's still the same fucking crowd. Different faces, sure, and different names to go with those faces, but really it was all the same. The energy, the spirit of that place hadn't changed. I

recognized the dive bar archetypes: the cool loner; the happy-go-lucky drunkard; the pool hustler; the sexy bartenders with the low-cut blouses and mile-long legs and that fuck-me smile that says "Come spend some money on me..."; a suspicious European tourist or two, clutching their fanny packs in front of them; the regular who'd been there too long and doesn't realize that groove he'd found is actually an alcoholic rut going on five years; the immigrant Mexicans with their Coronas with the lime slices slipped in; the successful Asian businessman making and receiving calls on his latest greatest doo-hickey cell phone in between shots of the best house whiskey, expensive suit, shiny black shoes, slapping down twenty-, hundred-dollar bills for all to see and be impressed with, and still, he goes home alone every night. I glanced around trying to pick out which one might have been me ten years ago. All of them, certainly, at one point or another.

There in the corner was the angry loner brooding, smoldering. Or pretending to. This is the same guy who earlier had jabbed me in the back with his pool cue as he was lining up to take his shot. He shot me a look. "Sorry." But the motherfucker wasn't sorry. That look in his eye was telling me to fuck off. Well, so be it Mr. Gray-haired Chinaman. Go on trying to act like Bruce Lee, trying to stand a certain way, trying to be cool and intimidating. You're in some fucked-up loser bar in the Tenderloin and no one gives a shit.

A small group of Mexicans were running the pool table, playing for drinks and having a good time, cool like mice, unafraid and unassuming, most of them probably here illegally, scrounging up livings working as dishwashers, janitors, busboys, prep cooks. The Korean bar girls pay them no mind except to take their money. They are everywhere, nowhere. They are the invisible help. A decade ago I learned to play pool with another group of Mexicans, one in particular. Eric and I sipped our beers and wondered what became of Jose, the greatest damn pool player this side of all the self-proclaimed hustlers, the so-called pool sharks, the drunken hotshots, the hotdogs, this side of Minnesota Fats himself. Jose could win games drunk as hell. Barely able to stand, he'd have to prop himself up with his pool cue in between shots. Then, when it was his turn to take a shot, he would get down low, eye level to the table, line it up, pump, and shoot. Sunk. Jose possessed an innate sense of geometry and angles and velocity. The same sort of expertise that a physicist would apply when trying to land a man on the moon, Jose seemed to possess naturally without any post-graduate degrees in physics or mathematics.

I wondered why he didn't turn pro or play in any of the money tournaments around the city. We'd seen him beat down so many guys night after night it wasn't even funny. But it eventually became clear why he never quite reached that level of competition.

He worked as a prep cook getting paid under the table at some mom-and-pop diner out in the trendy poseur wannabe Marina district. He worked till the early afternoon six days a week, which was the same for a lot of the other Mexicans who frequented that bar -- one day off, and the other six days, you're working ten-, twelve-hour shifts, making seven, eight bucks an hour. Tax-free, no health benefits, no sick time. One thing about those Mexicans, though, they were extremely generous. I would even say, self-less, with what little money they made, always offering to buy drinks, plunking down their own quarters for those games of pool, when they weren't hustling, that is.

When Jose's shift ended each day, from three o'clock onward, guaranteed you could find him perched atop his stool at the end of the bar, drinking Budweiser after Budweiser. Budweiser was his drink of choice while all the other Mexicans drank their Coronas with the lime wedges. Club-Med ain't the only place that's got 'em.

Every day, seven days a week, Budweiser upon Budweiser, for the two or three years that I was a regular there, Jose slowly drank his life away and pissing it all down that filthy barroom toilet. Just like the rest of us.

I was there every day, too. I'd roll in at about eight or nine. I could rarely hold out longer than that. I tried to force myself to stay home some evenings -- watch the baseball game, try some home-cooking for once -- but I wanted to be in a place where everyone knew my name. Well, some of them, anyway, so I'd slip on my Skinny Puppy baseball cap, slide into my leather jacket and head out the door. Drunks, all drunks. We were the low-life losers, the poor, the wretched. But it was more than that. We weren't yet laying in the gutter sipping hootch out of paper bags. There was hope for us yet. We each saw it, and we each recognized it for what it was. We were all loners, and we returned night after night to be a part of the crowd, to be a part of that giant sealed-off fishbowl of life, regulars co-mingling with lost tourists, shooting pool with the occasional lunatic that wanders in through those wide open doors. If you can survive for twenty-one years, you are allowed entry. That's the only requirement. No fat doorman at the door gauging your coolness, weighing your attractiveness. Exclusivity is for the insecure. Let it all in. We'll deal with it.

By the time I would get there, Jose was already shit-faced drunk, slouching over the bar, head resting literally in a pool of his own spittle, speech slurred, puke-stained breath. But get him over to the pool table, and he would shoot us down, one after the other -- bing bing bing. Next! Then stagger out into the night. Sometimes we'd wonder if we would see him the next day. One day we wouldn't. He was in love with the dayshift bartender, a fifty-plus-year-old Korean woman who wore her makeup in the tradition of Elvira, Mistress of the Dark. She worked her shift until seven each night, and when she quit, he did too. I never saw him after that. I wondered if he got deported. He always talked about going back home.

—

Every bar has its share of dirty old men. They keep to the shadows, peering out lasciviously, hunched over, sipping their girly drinks -- pina coladas, margaritas, bloody marys, wine coolers, various "lite" beers. They're not there to drink; they're there to cop a feel, get their nuts tickled, taking a short break from spending dollar bills in the strip club down the block or preying on underaged crack whores around the corner. The Korean bar girl struts up and down, working that bar, flimsy silky nighty for a top and short short skirts or Daisy Dukes, sweet perfume-scented, all smiles and light brushes across the hand like a feather as they hand you your change (what you think is left of it). The creepy old men wiggle like hooked worms in their seats, barely able to contain themselves. Some of them lean forward on the bar, like expectant schoolboys. It's all they can do to keep from lunging over the bar and having their way with one of those girls right there on the wet rubber-matted floor. I've had the same thoughts myself as has every other guy who may have wandered into that joint on a Friday or Saturday night. It's all a prick tease to loosen up those wallets, a practice that probably dates back to when man first realized that thinking with his dick could cost him a lot of money and threw it all away, anyway. Thus was born Lust and her wicked twin sister, centuries and centuries of Bitter Disillusionment.

Men outnumber the women five to one. The girls know this. They're surrounded like birds in a cage, yet they are the ones setting the trap. Their legs are closed and who knows what goes on in their minds. But nobody's paying any attention. The dirty old men sit there, mesmerized, leering. They think they are the ones in control with their wallets stuffed full of a trivial week's pay, but those Korean bar girls are as deft as pickpockets, much more adept and studied than the clumsy co-eds who work the strip clubs, bumping and gyrating and under the impression that fake tits and perfume bought at the Macy's counter is enough to get the job done. Korean chicks are smarter. They smile and laugh along knowing full well that fool and his money will soon be parted. At the end of the evening, you'll be left with a throbbing hard-on and no relief in sight. These are the poor saps who get tricked into purchasing a two-hundred dollar bottle of Exo, thinking it will buy their way into those silky tight Korean panties, but what they get is exactly what they paid for -- a bottle of overpriced whiskey and maybe a few turns on the karaoke machine in the back room. All the while, the girl sitting intimately close, smiling and laughing along, but -- no touch, no touch!

There was an old Korean man who used to visit every week or so, spending all his money in this fashion -- wasting it, as we all were, wildly and with abandon. One of the girls mentioned he was filthy rich. He owned businesses or apartments or something and could afford to blow four or five hundred a night. Fool. Other folks seemed impressed, in awe of his spending prowess. Uh, yeah. In some dive bar in the Tenderloin. That's like going to the dollar store on payday with your five hundred dollars: "Hey, you say everything's a dollar? Well, then. I'll buy five hundred things!" What a waste.

Then there was a detective who frequented the place and made it known short of advertising it on a neon sign outside the place that he was a detective out of the Taraval precinct out in the Avenues. He walked and acted like a cop. He didn't need a badge or uniform to tip anyone off. He strolled into the place with a confident swagger and a smirk that said, "I've got a gun and the authority to blow your fucking brains out." He'd stroll up to the bar and lean on one elbow, again, with that confident swagger. He reeked of old school corruption -- dead prostitutes, Chinese gangland payoffs, back alley deals with the local drug lords. Or maybe that was all just according to my own drunken imaginings. His fashion sense was a mix of Columbo reruns and John Gotti's glory days. In fact, he bore a passing resemblance to the latter, except shorter and not quite as dapper.

I noticed this same detective there tonight as Eric went to order another round. Same style, nothing changed, propped up against the bar with that one elbow and that smile which was still a condescending smirk.

—

22

Outside was the Tenderloin with her junkies, her homeless, lost tourists, and residents like small animals in the forest scurrying about on the forest floor; chipped neon signs and the swishing and swooshing of passing traffic. Was any of this planned? It almost seems accidental that this neighborhood ever came into being. There is that familiar stench of rotting food and stale urine wafting up from the streets, perspiring through its asphalt pores. In a sickly sense, this part of the city is alive, much like a tumor. It has the disturbing ability to grow its own teeth, its own hair, within the folds of its infected flesh. Indeed, it lives. It is like a scab that will never fully heal and can never be peeled. It is simply there to behold and to deal with.

This neighborhood was my home for many years. This is where I left the thin shell of adolescence behind and threw myself head first into the murky waters of adulthood. You can't learn to think for yourself when you're constantly worrying about what everyone else is thinking. I came to the city to leave all of that behind along with whatever notions I once had of myself. This city became my blank canvas and my little hidey-hole all at once. It became my retreat whenever I felt threatened, insecure, or whenever my station in life wasn't as stable as I'd first imagined. I come here to refocus, zero in on what it is I really need to be doing with my life.

Part of this process is to head out the door and just start walking, in any direction, at any time of day or night. I didn't realize it then, but walking was to become my primary form of meditation, to just go anywhere and just think by yourself. Only in some crowded city can you wander aimlessly on foot, you can observe the people, their comings and goings -- all of this done anonymously, through the safety of your own unfiltered thoughts. Cloaked in anonymity you have the freedom to be candid or the fool. There are no labels to hide behind. There is no pretending to be something you're not because nobody cares. And there's nothing to stop you from doing otherwise, either -- and still, nobody cares. Grow like a vine towards your own source of sunlight. I'm just some guy in an olive drab army jacket and baseball cap wandering the streets, anonymous, inconsequential, weak -- watching, listening, observing, then moving slowly and deliberately, like some half-baked Buddha. The Tenderloin became my own Walden Pond, except polluted and more like an oily puddle.

—

Eric and I finished our drinks then left. There was no point in staying for another. We were like ghosts, living in a past which no longer suited either of us. Another generation of alcoholics and no-life lowlifes had sprouted up in our stead, which is how it must be, how it's always been. These streets, these buildings, will never remember your name. Our lives pass like fragile wisps of smoke then quietly fade away. We bid each other good-bye on that noisy corner at Geary and Larkin and headed in opposite directions. He had to wake early the next morning for a class on teaching English as a second language. I headed for another bar down the street.

In earlier days I might have continued drinking until my vision blurred and staggering down the street wasn't possible without feeling my way along the wall. I'd wait for that familiar throbbing in my head and ears. My personality would change like the Incredible Hulk. Unlike the Hulk, I didn't grow stronger the drunker I got. Hulk is fiction, and I would still be stuck in my own painful reality. Things would be different this night. There would be no destructive rampaging or forsaking of the past and whatever obligations may have sprung from that -- marriage, fatherhood, a decent job with health benefits and all the free bottled water a guy could drink. I no longer felt comfortable playing the part of Kali the Destroyer, who destroys in order to create again. It was time to search for a new role.

I wandered into the place on Geary and Jones. It's a relatively sleepy spot, not as loud or active as the place I'd just left. The same Korean woman from years' past was working there tonight with that same droopy, hang-dog face. Her greeting was dubious at best, but I know she recognized me from before. A younger girl was working there, too. Eye candy. Beautiful, intelligent, spoke perfect English, but with a stare like an icepick through the chest. I kept my distance. There was no hard sell like at the other place. No tits and ass in your face with fake smiles and false interest in your miserable uninteresting life. This was more low-key, take it or leave it. They made little attempt at masking their contempt for the losers who came in through that old wooden door. For some reason, maybe due to its proximity to Union Square, the place gets more white customers (European tourists, mostly) than the other spots. Because of this, I've tended to avoid the place over the years. Too many tourists and not enough locals make for a dry boring evening, indeed -- khakis, fanny packs, leathery suntans, and strange European or Midwestern accents.

"Where ya from?" Ahh. "Whaddya do?" Yes, yes. "Nice to meetcha." "Take care." "In my country we do it this way and we call it that." Ahh, I see.

The old men regret bringing their flabby bird-like wives along and wish they could sneak out for a quick visit to one of those Asian massage parlors around the corner. Oh, the mistakes we men have made all in the name of lust. I would cave to no such temptations tonight. I downed my last drink for the evening and took a stroll up to North Beach.

—

Walking wherever and whenever. One of the beauties of being in a real city. This ability to meander and wander near or far, on foot, would be one of my top ten requisites if I were in charge of determining a city's worth as a true, world-class city or if it's just some bullshit pretender, a hob-nob collection of strip malls, chain restaurants, and artsy-fartsy shops that sell doilied crap that no one buys, except old ladies and other artsy-fartsy shop owners. The streets must be narrow, asphalt chipped and broken down, only good for walking with no room for cars or trucks; no expressways or freeway on-ramps or six-lane thoroughfares; no crosswalks where pedestrians have to sprint a quarter-mile to make it to the other side or risk being run over by assholes gunning their engines waiting for the light to turn green; a liquor/grocery store or deli/market on every corner; a varied collection of people living together on the same block, every block, and not just a bunch of monotonous hard-ons in Dockers khakis with perky-breasted girlfriends in tow, the ones with the nasally whines, searching for the nearest sports bar; a city where tourists are treated with contempt and not encouraged to be like idiots (see Las Vegas, Disneyland), a city that doesn't need them to survive (New York City, for example); a city where celebrities go to hide and not be seen, where they can relax in blissful anonymity like the rest of us. Hollywood is for teenage girls or those suffering from similar youthful afflictions.

I would rather see a barren wasteland before me than some grotesque eyesore like Las Vegas or Orange County or Pleasanton, California. Forget about bombing Iraq. We ought to aim those guided lasers back at ourselves and blast away at those monuments to architectural stupidity and equally stupid city planning and engineering, where everything is designed around the automobile and the assumption that we, as dumbfuck Americans, are willing to drive five miles down the road for that gallon of cookie dough ice cream or bag of Doritos. Tell that to the 90-year-old lady with poor eyesight and a shaky grip who's got to get behind the wheel and drive down to the pharmacy to pick up her prescription. Suddenly that car becomes a two-ton death machine as she maneuvers it down city streets. Hide the women and children! Here comes Grandma! Get off the sidewalk! Here she comes! That will be all of us some day. I don't want to be the guy who's got to catch a bus forty-five minutes uptown just so I could pick up another pack of adult diapers, praying to God I don't lose my bowels along the way. If I'm going to shit my pants, I'd rather do it in the privacy of my own home.

—

The stroll from the Tenderloin to North Beach isn't very far -- maybe a mile or two at the most -- hardly treacherous; the path is lined with tourists, late-night office workers, lawyers and bankers from the financial district entertaining clients. I find it peculiar to see rich old men out and about on a Friday night, like frat boys out there having fun, laughing out loud and confidently, as they stroll down the darkened lamp-lit streets. Their laughter sounds more sinister than joyous. Shouldn't they be home in their mansions tucked away safe and warm? Shouldn't they be preparing their last will and testament and atoning for their sins? Have all their years of success commanding men and companies made them confident in their old age that they would overcome it, that in all their material wealth, they have become like gods themselves and can laugh defiantly in the face of their Maker? This is the laugh of one born into privilege and expects it. Hard work has nothing to do with it. You could work your ass off at McDonald's for ten years, full time, making six-fifty an hour, and at the end of that decade you'll have enough saved up to buy a couple of cheeseburgers and a large order of fries. Fifty bucks a day. Not bad if you're living rent-free and you don't need to eat.

I'm hiking up through Chinatown now, making my way up Grant Street. The shops are closed, and the tourists have left. It's dark. All the years I lived in S.F., and I've never been up this way this late in the evening. In the distance, I can still hear the old rich men laughing, like slave-traders and devils. On the opposite side of the street, I see an old Chinese man making his way home, hunched over, beat down, tired, and sad looking. He's alone with his pink Chinatown plastic bag, the kind every Chinatown shop hands you when you've purchased a handful of their goodies. In the bag he carries tonight's dinner, leftovers from today's lunch. When he gets home, he'll reheat those pork noodles or that fried duck with rice that has hardened into little bits of plastic. Too tired to even remove his stained white smock, he wears it all the way home, reeking of fish, chicken guts, and back alley garbage cans. If these Chinatown streets were still crowded, tourists would be swerving to avoid him. It's good that he comes home so late at night, he thinks to himself. Spare him the humiliation of trudging through the suspicious, judgmental crowds. "Look, momma! Is that a real Chinaman?" "Yes, dear." "Ew, he smells like fish!" "Don't get too close now." In the distance, the old white men are still laughing.

From Grant, I cut over to Columbus and stroll past Vesuvio and City Lights Books. Nothing here now but poseurs and more tourists gawking at the posing poseurs, standing around staring at each other like weird beetles. The bookstore itself is always worth a visit, likewise the one a few doors down from the Condor on Broadway at the top of Kearny. The Beats are dead. They've been beat down and ground into a pulpy mass for mass consumption, little bite-sized chunks of rebellion for all the sensitive poets sniffing rose petal farts in creative writing classes. Slap a black beret on this shit and bury it already. Roll up a copy of the New Yorker and shove it down those pink cocksucker throats. There is no writing like a dying man whose guts have spilled onto the streets after he's blown himself up. Who? Please tell me, who?

I'm not book-shopping tonight or any night for the foreseeable future. There's an entire bookshelf of books sitting at home that I have yet to read. I'm buying them faster than I can read them. And there's an empty bookshelf that I haven't yet purchased that I plan to fill with all the books I hope to write. The two bookshelves of opposing forces are constantly warring upon another, and I'm stuck in the middle, paralyzed. Tonight I'm just walking, just passing through. Looking at everything and looking for nothing. Wear down that slight feeling of drunkenness before I head back to my room in the Tenderloin. Walk off the drunkenness, and along with it, the bad feelings, the jealousy, the insecurity, the hopelessness, the defeat that I'd been feeling recently.

I weave through the happy, eager crowds, immortal in their youth, and realize how I've aged. How the years have sped by, unseen and anonymous. I am content in my own silence, my quiet solitude. I no longer feel a need to meet anyone but myself, don't succumb to that pressure of being part of the crowd -- amongst them, yes, but not a part of them. It feels nice to disappear into it, amidst all that noise, the chatter, the traffic with the beep-beep honking horns, the music wafting out of restaurant windows and barroom doorways, young women excited to be spending a night out with their friends and boyfriends. Was a time when I was in awe of such people, when I felt intimidated by them, their happy lives and the bright futures that lay before them. I wondered, what was the secret, what was this thing they possessed, which I seemed to be lacking, that enabled them to feel so confident and certain of their station in life? But good looks fade, small fortunes are squandered, and that certainty in life might very well lead to boredom, monotony and secret addictions to painkillers. Failure, of course, is the best teacher. Better a three-time loser than some sentimental fool whose glory days are frozen in the past. Losers will always have something to look forward to, even if it is the mere thought of escaping the present. Poor today, hopefully not so poor tomorrow. But you got to try.

I looped around North Beach Pizza and headed back down Kearny. North Beach on weekend nights is the same it's always been -- crowded with people from the East Bay and surrounding suburbs. Suburban kids trying to look and act older than the minimum drinking age. Must be all the neon signs and crowds that attract them, like squirrels to nuts and old people to Vegas casinos. You feel drawn to all the excitement and that orgy of activity. The energy, the crowds, all that buzzing busy-ness that is often mistaken for life itself, people milling about trying to keep busy, doing things, anything, if only to say the following Monday that they did something over the weekend, anything to occupy themselves in that mad vacuum of space and time, when all you really need to do is just sit and be still. Be silent and observe like a quiet mouse in the forest. Everything else is the ego trying to assert itself. You must reach in and strangle it. Murder it. Obliterate it. Smash it into tiny pieces and grind it to dust beneath the heel of your foot. The ego is the reason for all the assholes, the jerks, and motherfuckers out there in the world. It is why we fought two world wars and every war before or since. The ego says "All is mine. Vengeance is mine." It struts about, an out-of-control throbbing hard-on, bumping into everything, stumbling over its own testicles. Any perceived threat to its existence must be dealt with swiftly, violently, without compassion, common sense, or any semblance of reason. The ego says "You are weak, and I am strong." The ego says "I am faster, smarter, better, and you, you are the loser. You are not worthy. I pass judgment upon you, and you are unworthy to stand beside me and partake in the warm glow which is my own glory." The ego is vanity and jealousy all at once. It is hatred and lust, snide smirks and mean-spirited comments. It is lord and master of the crowded night. The ego fills the room and leaves nothing of any value in its wake.

—

My feet were beginning to tire from all the walking I'd been doing, around town and downtown. It had been a long day. I didn't get much sleep the previous night waiting and worrying for Nadjet to come home at two, or was it three, in the morning. Then with jealous, insecure feelings I went into work, feeling like a pile of shit the entire day, email meaningless, test planning meaningless, a decent job at one of the best tech companies meaningless. Code reviews, test results, debugging and troubleshooting -- were nothing more than balls of lint tucked away in the corners of my mind, the great big empty halls of my mind, lonely footstep echoes all sad and gloomy.

Some people can escape into their work when they're feeling beat down and attacked, but not me and not with this kind of job, the meaningless, pointless kind, the kind that only pays the rent and provides a dim hope of more years of corporate servitude to follow, the kind that gets you spinning your wheels and firing your cylinders, but still, you get nowhere. Some go along willingly, gleefully, excited at the job title printed beneath their name on their business cards. Go forward, young man, and be proud to be ground into hamburger. Engineers fresh from India with their Wal-Mart slacks and Target buttoned-down shirts, still showing the creases from the factory fold, hurl themselves willingly into the mix. Now is their time to shine and make a name for themselves. Everyone will know that Gopal Ragamadishalan wrote the bit of code that went into the feature that went into the software that runs that little square box sitting on a rack down in the server room that enables Suzy Jones, admin assistant in the tight skirt, to update her MySpace blog site from her cube at work without her boss's knowledge, who in turn, is using that same bit of code to cruise porn sites on the sly with the door to his office closed as if he were huddled in there on a very important conference call.

Everyone wants to be brilliant. Everyone wants to be a genius. They must teach this in every school in India. They've studied all the brilliant geniuses who have come before them -- Einstein, Bill Gates, Steve Jobs, the CEOs of all the Fortune 500 companies. They relate anecdotes from the lives of these men as if from rote memory, as if they were parables or Bible stories. Gandhi is frowned upon, his name muttered with a smirk. He was not a capitalist.

In baseball parlance, these guys want to be on the team that goes all the way to the World Series. Very few will ever get beyond Double-A ball. Aside from the pioneering ones who came and made their mark, the rest are poorly made clones of the original, possessing the demeanor of robots, not champions. Me, I'm the bat-boy looking for a way out. I might take a few swings for the fence during batting practice, but that's the extent of my involvement. Let the other guys be the stars, albeit in their own minds, writing that slick piece of code, finding that gnarly bug that would have brought our biggest customer to their knees. Everything seems to be done with "visibility" in mind -- visibility to upper management, visibility to the rest of the team. In other words, they want to be known, they want to be recognized. Am I the only one who prefers to work under the radar? There can be no real glory in toiling away at work that can be done by trained monkeys or robots. Your only rewards are more work and an implied, but legally unenforceable, promise of continued employment. Dumbfuck newbies fall for it every time, myself included. It is only when you tire of the work and that gut-churning feeling of unfulfillment remains that you realize maybe quitting that mailroom job all those years ago for another gig that paid a buck-fifty more wasn't such a good idea after all. Should've kept it simple.

—

I find myself at the Chinatown playground across from the Holiday Inn on Kearny. There is a swimming pool on the roof of that hotel. We snuck up there once when we were teenagers -- me, my brother Andre, and our friend Larry. We had each dropped a hit of acid on the train ride into the city about an hour earlier. In the pool area on the roof of the hotel twenty-seven stories up, a sign greeted us: No Swimming. I picked it up and hurled it over the ledge. We leaned over and watched as it careened off the side of the building, then spun around and drooped down into the middle of the street just like a giant ace of spades. It came to rest with a dull, anti-climactic "kl-klang".

Back on the street, we watched a giant wrecking ball tear away at an old brick building. It was evening and they had the demolition zone covered in floodlights. The giant ball came around again and -- WHAM -- it slammed into the side of the building. Bricks, dust, and bits of debris came crumbling down. To my slightly hallucinating mind, the falling pieces took on the appearance of bodies falling out of windows, then flashed back to shadowy debris. I tried to watch more closely in hopes of spotting more bodies and warn the construction crew that, hey, there were people still in there, but my brother was having another kind of hallucination.

"I feel wet."

"You're not wet. You're tripping."

"Touch me. Don't I feel wet?"

"Dude, you're not wet."

"Feels like I'm wet."

"Well, you're not."

This continued every few minutes, and each time we had to assure him that no, he most definitely was not wet.

I was left wondering about the falling bodies. Many years later I would watch a similar scene unfold on live television as the World Trade Center towers came crashing down -- bodies falling out of windows like so much debris. I remember watching a black guy in a three-piece suit succumb to his fate as he let himself fall from a highrise window. He sort of just tumbled like a crash-test dummy. When he left for work that morning, did he have some clue, some hint or vibe that he would never see his wife and kids again, that he would never know that feeling of relief upon returning home after another fucked up day at the office? Maybe he didn't like his job. Maybe he was planning to quit. Perhaps he was sitting at his desk, daydreaming of a better existence. And yet there he was, alone in his office, throwing himself from the window. Post-It notes, desk, chair, computer, scattered papers -- the last things he sees before hurling himself into the abyss, his final witnesses. My dreams the next few nights were filled with the cries and moaning of the people who had died and those who lay buried in the rubble. It started as a distant whisper, then slowly grew louder inside my head until I awoke and thought I was hearing it right there in our bedroom.

The events from that day recede further and further into the past, coming up on five years now as I write this. How things have changed and how much they haven't depends on your frame of mind, I suppose. For me, the battle has always been more of an internal nature. Not changing the world but changing how I see the world. All wars begin with an internal seed of hatred and anger. Look at Hitler, Napoleon, Osama bin Laden, George fucking Bush. A single man with a certain hatred. Their own personal hatreds and flaws manifest into cultural hatreds and flaws. These seeds are spread and cultivated from individual to individual, generation to generation. It all begins with one man and a will to force everyone else to see things his way. HIS way. It's all ego and no life. It spreads like disease and atrophy. Dreams die. Lives waste away. Cultures fade and disappear. There is no hope, no art where there is no creation, no hope for the individual being itself. Ego doesn't create, it destroys slowly. It eats away like termites on rotting wood. It is the psychological manifestation of cancer. Nothing thrives. War is the result of ego. All those fuckers out there in the world -- they thrive like tumors on the brain.

Me versus myself. Self meeting self, as Edgar Cayce once put it. Why blow shit up if the problem is within yourself, your own psyche, your own flawed interpretation of other people and perhaps even of your own faith? How do you know? Fact is, you don't, and until you do, you should keep your mouth shut, keep your head down, and trudge along through your own miserable life. Nobody's fault but mine, ought to be our collective mantra. All fingers point back at you. All roads lead inward. This absolute belief in your own righteousness is nothing more than fucked up delusion. Judging what's right and wrong is not up to the individual. The point of life is to simply live it and go your own way. Live our own lives and not point fingers. The great cosmic balance is achieved on its own. It hardly needs the assistance of man -- weak, puny, and unworthy in all our glorious stupidity. We are like tiny insects caught up in an ocean swell -- folly to think we could ever control it.

And this is why I find myself in some Chinatown park on a Friday night, alone, insecure and trying to hear the answer, any answer, whispered my way on some cosmic wind. Whenever I find myself confronting problems with no obvious solution, I like to go off on my own, wander around, let everything simmer and stew for a bit. I need to be alone, get away from all the things that seem to be pushing me this way, pulling me that way. All the little things that needle away at me, poke and prod me, expecting, requiring my involvement, like a thousand racquet balls I've smacked out in every direction and now they're bouncing back my way, hurtling twice as fast. This is my idea of karma. And then: Oh, shit -- what the hell do I do now?

I.

Don't.

Know.

Some guys hold themselves out to be experts of one thing or another by the time they reach my age. I'm 36-years-old. What the hell do I know? I'm still bumbling about, struggling with the written word, trying to find an easier way to pay the rent. Pro ball-players are nearing retirement after years of making good money playing a game they love. Lawyers are being made into partners. Med students are becoming doctors. Writers already have a few books and articles under their belts. Talking heads on the news channels prop themselves up as being experts on one subject or another: terrorism, finance, nutrition, whatever -- names and fancy titles flashing on a banner beneath their blabbing mouths.

I suppose this is what it means to have a career -- at some point you become an expert at what you do. And then you are expected to share your expertise. Bestow it upon those less knowledgeable. To nod like a gentle understanding parent when approached by eager acolytes and understudies: Yes, I know more than you. Yes, I too made the same idiotic mistakes.

And if you are content with simply sitting around daydreaming, doing absolutely nothing from day to day, then surely you will become an expert at being yourself. Or perhaps wandering aimlessly about, comparing this stone to that stone, the shapes of clouds and unseen wind patterns, how the tall grass bends and sways while never really losing its form. What else have you got to think about, otherwise, if not your own thoughts, your own little quirks, the way you walk, the way you lift a cup of coffee to your lips, how you perceive the light and the shadows as they pass through the leaves of a tree? You sit, you ruminate, you rediscover memories long since forgotten like smooth, round pebbles stored in a box over the years. You will learn infinite patience and the art of sitting still and keeping silent.

—

I sit in that Chinatown park on one of the benches in the dark, quietly. I spot a few slumped over shadows across the ways -- homeless snuggled in for the night. In the daytime, this place is crowded with Chinatown kids and old Chinese men playing Chinese boardgames, but they've all gone to bed in their respective Chinatown hovels, an impenetrable collection of tenement apartments that sit above the shops and restaurants and Chinatown barbershops and back-alley fortune cookie bakeries. You'll never find any of these places advertised for rent in any English-speaking newspaper. At least, I've never come across any. In Chinatown, Americans are the foreigners.

A row of hedges mark the boundary of the park and act as a divider which keeps us hidden from the people walking down the sidewalk. From the other side, I hear a young woman laughing with her friends. Across the street at the hotel, another group of people wait outside laughing and having a good time. I sit, listening. It would drive me mad to be homeless and to sit on that park bench day upon day, week after week, listening, seeing all the happiness, the normalcy, around me -- separated by an invisible wall, stewing in my own filth and hunger, knowing I could not be a part of it even if I'd wanted. All just sadness and rejection, being blocked out like a shadow, like cast out spirits. I suppose you'd learn to tune it out after a while. You become numb to it. You begin to believe that you are not human. Inhuman, you become accustomed to being treated like something worse than the family pet, worse than an animal running about in the wild. You begin to feel that you deserve the filth and squalor of living out on the streets. At what point do you forget the human spirit and let it die within you? Or does it merely lie dormant, waiting to be reawakened?

The alcoholic buzz has settled in. Whenever I close my eyes, I feel the pulse of my heartbeat throbbing in my ears. And the laughter all around of people enjoying a Friday night. Well-fed privileged kids from the suburbs, perfumed stank and false bravado. Teenagers and twenty-somethings out on the town. I am wary of them. The homeless I can understand and empathize with. They've been beat down and humbled, forced to grovel or dig through trash cans for the leftover crumbs and slightest bits of scraps. Society has cast them out and yet they exist within its folds and hide within its creases. At some point in their lives, some of them may have been just like these kids tonight -- confident in their youth, reckless, careless, invincible. Their smiles might very well have been just as wide and infinite as the universe, their laughter echoing throughout the cosmos. But now they sit hunched over in some abandoned park -- the children have gone home for the evening, the old men have gone home to wait another day for death. Only the homeless remain. They drift in like fallen leaves to claim the cold dark places. Sheer will and the breath of God within them is what keeps them alive. They don't have nice houses or fancy cars or nine-to-five jobs to pay for all of it. Their clothes are greasy oily rags found at the bottom of dumpsters; their faces sunburnt, cracked and creased; muscles sore, feet swollen. The act of bending to sit is painful and brings little relief. How close they are to knowing God, Buddha, Jesus, Mohammed! They know hunger, deprivation. They know the feeling of being cast out and despised. They know failure, pain, long-suffering. All that was once in their possession has been stripped away. What remains is that which brings them closest to God, which makes them like Gods themselves, and they are humbled. All of them -- the drunkards, the confused maniacs, the Vietnam vets, the schizophrenic heroin addicts, the black guys from Missouri -- all of them. They may have lost their minds, each and every one of them, but they haven't lost their souls. They might have lost families, fortunes, limbs. Rise up! Bow down and accept your karma, your miserable fates, your death sentences for life strung out over hours, days and years. And in all your misery and in spite of it, learn to see the glory of the morning sun and recognize the majesty of that which makes you human.

The kids -- the teenagers and the twenty-somethings -- haven't yet realized this. They're still invincible, immortal, unkillable. They don't yet know the pain of childbirth or the pain of having to pay for it without medical insurance, having to pay rent, mortgages, car payments, or having to show up for work every day, day in, day out, rain or shine with a boss who can't wait to shove his boot up your ass and the coworker who can't wait to provide the assist. The future of which they are vaguely aware is only that which they've read or heard about from other people -- a friend's older brother who went into the navy, their dad who's worked as a lawyer/carpenter/banker all his adult life, a girlfriend or boyfriend who's got a cousin who moved to Hollywood to chase that superficial dream or maybe joined that punk rock band to tour the country in a rundown cargo van. Rumors, hearsay, dull expectations. That "go ahead and see for yourself" reality hasn't yet arrived with its dim baggage and gloomy clouds. Glory and fame lie just around the corner. There'll be no drudgery or monotony for them! They can do anything and will indulge themselves willingly. Stupidity and the risk of death or dismemberment don't register in their young minds. They only know fun and excitement and the adrenaline rush that those things provide. So they'll race down crowded streets going ninety miles an hour. They'll set fire to that homeless guy in the doorway. They'll smash windows and vandalize cars. They will fight and harass people on the streets. They'll fuck and breed without knowing how to raise and nurture. There is nothing more dangerous than a marauding band of bored teenagers. I know what they can do because I've often done the same and failed just as miserably.

I retreat behind the hedge in that lonely Chinatown park and rest my tired feet. Slightly hungry, slightly buzzed. I close my eyes again. So peaceful, so calm. It is a beautiful cool evening. I rest my head against my chest and almost fall asleep. In all my years, I think I've slept outside maybe once in my life. 1983. Family reunion on the island of Oahu in Hawaii. All of us kids were sleeping in tents out on the beach. My grandfather had taken us spear-fishing out along the shallows earlier that evening. We caught nothing. We stabbed and jabbed at anything that moved just beneath the surface and only ended up cutting our feet upon the sharp coral. I realized then that I could never be a true native Hawaiian like my dad or my grandfather or any of my cousins or uncles who were all good swimmers and surfers and stuck their chests out all macho and tough, talking that tough Hawaiian talk, pidgin English style. So why even try? I was born in Hayward, California. The beach and that vast saltwater ocean were as alien to me at the time as girls and New York City. A good twenty years have passed and I can say with confidence that not much has changed.

I began to nod off. The cool evening and my own weariness lulled me. More crackling laughter across the street jolted me awake. Would I be able to spend the entire night out there? I hadn't planned on it, but the notion appealed to me. This idea of voluntary homelessness was not an alien one. It has occupied my thoughts for some time now. I'd say the last ten years or so. I wondered if I could live so ascetically. Could I wander this continent, the world even, like the hobos, the punks, the tramps, the teenage runaways? Could I live like the worms and beetles tucked away in the soft earth? What would it feel like to sit on that park bench forever? To quietly retreat into myself, hear and feel the silent implosion of my own universe. Before the shell of my body is allowed to crumble and blow away as dust, there must be hunger, thirst, migraine headaches, and involuntary spasms. A dissolution of the attachment to the physical self. I soil myself and still I do not move from my place on the bench. Pigeons come to rest upon my shoulder. They defecate on me. My skin dries, then sags, then tightens against the bones in my face, tightens like leather about my skull. I am alone, and my breathing is shallow. I sink deeper and deeper within myself, like looking up from the bottom of a deep deep well, my soul.

More laughter from across the street. I open my eyes and spot a shadow shuffling about across the way. The homeless slumps of men stretched along the other benches toss and turn. They are still human. They can still see, hear, and smell the same things. They share the same sidewalks, breathe the same air. Though they might not have eaten in the last three days, they are not allowed to taste the food they cannot afford to buy. Though they might hear the laughter and understand the jokes, they are not allowed to participate in any conversation with people who are cleaner, more well-dressed than them. If they look at anything it is from a sidelong glance, a quick stab of a stare from within the shadows looking out toward a bright noonday sun. European tourists wrinkle their noses with disdain. There is not a kind eye amongst this lot. They are a suspicious bunch, clutching their purses, their Nordstrom's bags, their fanny packs. Centuries of Mongol and Moorish and Turkish invasions have taught them to be wary of that thing around the corner that will come to kick the shit out of them. It will arrive with certainty, and with certainty it will again kick the shit out of them. Centuries of being on the losing side of all the raping and pillaging and maiming have embedded this in the European mindset. They're expecting it. Not if, but when will it happen? Catastrophe, plague, grown men crying and flailing about, running down ash-covered streets in stained tighty-whities. Entire families slaughtered. Generations gone in the blink of an eye.

To be forced to live outside in the urban elements means more than sleeping on wet pavement, begging for change, or finding a quiet spot to lose your bowels. You've got to deal with the hatred, the contempt, being ignored and avoided. When you sleep you've got to watch for gangs of teenagers looking to light you up with a bit of gasoline and a match. Some may come merely to kick you in the head. Others may hurl empty beer bottles at you as they drive down the street. Or fire upon you with pellet guns or worse. Lack of shelter and food are the last of your concerns when you tuck in for the night. Being homeless is being vulnerable. I would imagine. I can only imagine. It would take great courage to embrace it willingly, with wide open arms and wide-eyed wonder.

I have a wife and kid at home. They have no idea where I am tonight. I left home in a hurry, angry and insecure. I left my cell phone on the desk because I knew they would try to call. I escaped to the city to be nobody. But that isn't true.

I stood up and walked back to my hotel.

After the rains, the ground is damp and soft. The meadows I'm used to seeing in drier periods are flooded now and have become ponds. Egrets resting on branches in the distance take flight as I approach. A hawk circles high overhead. There is no sound but the wind's gentle lull and unknown birds in the distance chirping and cawing.

The path leads me along the edge of a farmer's property. The cows stare me down, probably mistaking me for a coyote or bobcat. Paw prints and deer tracks crisscross the trail the entire way. The cows soon realize that I am no threat -- quite useless, in fact -- and return to their bovine ways.

Even out here in these wide open spaces, you remain in my thoughts. I came to clear my mind, and yet....it's as if you accompany me along these grassy paths, strolling beside me. Tiny flowers bloom in unexpected places along the way, and I smile because I know it would also make you smile. I leave them be and avoid trampling them with my clumsy heavy-booted feet.

It is a meditative stroll, unhurried. I'm not interested in making time or mileage today. I've hiked this route before. It's only six miles over relatively easy rolling terrain. It usually takes me two hours to complete. I couldn't care if it took me twice that amount of time today. Today I am merely walking, daydreaming, and basking in the wonderful idea that women like you exist in the world.

I take my lunch in my usual spot -- a knoll along the rounded bend near the railroad tracks. Lunch is hummus spread over a tortilla with two slices of salami. I've made three such rolls prior to leaving earlier in the morning. I eat one and save the rest for later. Nothing fancy. Just something simple to give me enough energy to carry on.

Afterward, thinking to complete the remaining hike in calm reverie, I encounter a slow-moving tide of muddy brown water that was once a dry riverbed. Ah, of course. A riverbed becomes a river when the rains come. I spend a good half-hour trying to find some way across, bush-whacking in knee-high brambles, dead branches, and tall grass tangled with thorns. The forest canopy in this section is thick, and I struggle alone in the shade and shadows. I'm almost certain a deer spying from a safe distance or an owl in the trees witnessed my hapless struggling and said, "What an idiot."

I give up and turn back. But still I smile, knowing you were there with me in my thoughts.

"Hunting season? You serious?"

The guy loading fishing gear into the back of his truck is laughing at me. "Be careful, brudda."

He had asked if I was there to go deer hunting. I told him I was just planning to go for a walk. I feel ridiculous standing there now with my ski pole hiking stick and my backpack packed with little hummus and cheese tortilla wraps while everyone else is loading shotguns with #4 buckshot and gearing up to kill stuff. He is still laughing and shaking his head when he drives off.

It is hunting season at Hagerman Wildlife Refuge. I should have guessed as much judging by the number of gun-racked Ford F-150s parked along the road and filling up the small gravel parking lot. I've never seen it this crowded. The place is going to be filled with a bunch of Elmer Fudd wannabes today.

Damn.

I had already driven an hour to get to this place, my own little private isolated patch of forest out here in the middle of nowhere. Only the birds singing to me, grasshoppers following along, hawks circling far overhead. The place where I thought no human footprints other than my own ever came to tread. A place where I could go to compose pretty little poetry in my head and think beautiful Zen-like thoughts.

Not today. Today things will die if the Elmer Fudds have their way. I toss my pack into the back of the truck and head for Lake Texoma near the Oklahoma border, another hour's drive north.

But I don't mind. It's not like driving in the Bay Area, where you're constantly struggling and fighting stop-and-go traffic, assholes cutting you off, merging, stopping, speeding up, cutting across four lanes to get to your exit. In these parts of Texas, the roads are as open as the blue skies and roll out to the horizon. The drive itself is part of my enjoyment when I'm heading to these out-of-the-way places for a few hours of walking. I use the time to catch up on my music and my sanity. Driving is my own special way of doing that meditation head-clearing thing. These Texas roads readily lend themselves to such pastimes. Stricken by such moods, I have at times found myself wandering around small towns in West Texas or down south in San Antonio, much to my wife's surprise and consternation.

—

I'm heading to the Cross Timbers Trail on the Texas side of Lake Texoma. To get there, you head north on 377 and make a left on Cotton Mill Road. This road winds through a little neighborhood containing some of the funkiest looking, brightly painted ramshackle houses I've not seen anywhere outside of Berkeley, California. Code enforcement officers and building inspectors would have a field day with this place.

One house -- a wooden shack, really -- sits perched atop four purple-painted, twenty-foot-long, steel poles like an oversized birdhouse. It teeters haphazardly and a little lopsided over the neighboring shacks. On the front lawn of another house a crude hand-painted sign reads "Welcome to Fantasyland" with a crudely drawn arrow pointing to a beat-up looking front door. Across the street another hand-painted sign reads "Driveway to Nowhere," in obvious reference to Sarah Palin's "Bridge to Nowhere." One lot simply contains a trailer parked next to what appears to be a toolshed made out of scrap wood. In fact, many of the dwellings here have that scrap wood home-made look, stuff banged together using only hammers and a few nails. Architectural plans? Building contractors? Pshaw!

The roads are narrow and severely sloped. The place must be a mess when the rains come.

—

I pull up to the trailhead and park along the side of the road as the signs instruct. I see a troop of boy scouts loaded down with 40-pound packs about to head in the same direction that I'm planning to take. They're probably headed for Eagle's Roost, a camping spot two or three miles up the trail. I wait in the truck a while and give them a fifteen-minute head start. Fifteen minutes later, I catch up to them standing in the middle of the trail trying to figure out how to "sound off."

"Sound off again!"
"ONE!"
"TWO!"
"Uh, three?"

It's annoying whenever there are boy scouts on the trail. Always yelling, bantering, counting off -- ONE! TWO! THREE! Troop leaders shouting orders and barking like drill sergeants. How can you learn to appreciate the forest if you don't know how to go about, quietly listening?

They make room for me on the trail and I pass amongst them. "Hey! That's a pointy looking walking stick you got there." says one of the boys, mocking the two-dollar thrift store ski pole I use as a hiking stick. I smile and keep moving. You poor, chubby little child. In a few short years you will be lusting after young women, and they will ignore you and break your heart. You are better off remaining lost here in the forest. You will not realize this until you are my age and have seen the bottom of many a whiskey bottle. Good luck.

I encounter another troop about a mile onward. Their leader is looking at a topo map and glancing up at a tall tree, as if the tree is going to tell him which way to go. The tree doesn't care, nor does it appear on any topo map. A boy scout must always be prepared! Don't forget the condoms and liquor! These pedophiles get a little frisky in nighttime tents! I leave this troop to suffer their confusion. All the trails follow the lake's edge. It is not possible to get lost. On your way up, keep the lake to your right. On the way back, keep the lake to the left. You don't need a map for that. It's not like you're in the Alaskan wilderness with grizzlies chasing you down and Sarah Palin shooting at you from a helicopter above. Just follow the lake!

These snarky little comments I'm working over in my mind cause me to miss my own freeway exit. I miss the spot beneath a patch of trees overlooking the lake where I like to take a short break and rest up before starting the walk back. But it's autumn and fallen leaves blanket the ground, obscuring the trail in many parts.

I wander off-trail lost for a few minutes. I'm not too concerned. The path reveals itself in subtle ways, if only you tilt your head this way or that, or glance at things from a certain angle. The sunlight filtering through the forest canopy sprinkles the leafy-cushioned ground and I can just barely make out the indentations of all those who have gone before me. Always as they have gone before, so shall they go again. I merely follow.

I'm on the Lost Loop Trail, I finally realize. I follow it back to the main path and head home.

Sometimes people make mistakes.

I sit in my study with my glass of wine considering the ones that I have made over the years. Then I consider the one that she is making right now, while I sit in my study with my glass of wine.

—

The kid comes up to me and asks, "Daddy, if you had to pick your favorite cake, what would it be? Vanilla or chocolate?"

"Oh, I don't know," I say. "Why do you ask?"

Her smile is bright and mischievous. "I don't know! I'm just wondering."

"I guess I like chocolate better."

"Okay!" She runs away giggling.

The kid was excited about my birthday. That previous weekend, while I went my way and the wife went hers, the kid spent all her time planning and scheming for this magnificent event. She was very sly about it. It was supposed to be a secret, after all, and I was to know nothing about it. Even though she had sent me to the store to buy all the necessary supplies. I kind of had an idea what to expect.

Later as I'm paying the bills and examining all those heart-breaking phone records, the kid comes in again: "Daddy, what color combination do you like better -- green and orange, red and green, or blue and orange?"

"Oh, I don't know. Why do you ask?"

"I'm just wondering."

"Well, hmm. I suppose I like green and orange the best."

She runs off giggling again. "Thank you!"

Later that afternoon, I pass her in the living room. She is furiously scribbling away at something.

"Don't look this way!" she says. "I'm making you a surprise birthday card."

"Oh, okay," I say.

And of course, she presents me with my surprise a few minutes later: a hand-drawn birthday card on green and orange paper. I will save this one in a special file where I keep all the others that I have saved over the years. In this file, there are mermaids, dragons, dinosaurs, Happy Birthday cards, Valentine's cards, Father's Day and

Mother's Day cards, super heroes, fashion designs, stick figures and crayon figures. There are some cards that have even been sewn with colorful yarn and buttons. There is also a 50-page picture book, created using markers and crayons, which she had started when she was five or six years old. The book's protagonist is someone named the Evil Queen Mictoria.

Monday is my birthday, and I awaken alone. Another awkwardly formal affair with the wife rushing off to work while I try to get that first cup of coffee. No good-bye kiss for me. Again. Then I take a sleepy-eyed kid to school an hour later.

I treat myself to lunch at my favorite Japanese restaurant. I don't tell anyone it's my birthday. No one gives a shit. To some people, it's a big deal and they feel this annoying need to send out emails to everyone at work and make grand birthday pronouncements. I don't give a shit, either.

Later that evening at home, we have dinner. The kid and I eat at the kitchen table. The wife eats in the living room in front of the TV.

I get ready for bed. The kid comes into the room and wants me to read her favorite poem from "Where the Sidewalk Ends." She smiles widely as she turns the pages. "No, not this one. Not this one, either. Don't worry, I'll find the poem I want you to read!"

My eyelids are getting heavy. I'm getting sleepy. I think to myself, "Why does she always wait until bedtime to have me read poems or long passages from her chapter books?"

The wife yells something from the kitchen, something requiring my immediate attention. What now? A leak? A spider? Dogshit on the floor?

"What?" I go to the kitchen with the kid following close behind.

There are times when I'm a very slow thinker and fail to grasp the obvious, especially when I'm exhausted and can only think about sleep and where I might be sleeping in the foreseeable future.

All the lights had been turned off and then -- SURPRISE! -- there on the kitchen table is my chocolate birthday cake complete with burning wax candle numbers "3" and "8." I blow out the flames, and the child is laughing and smiling bright. She is so happy to see me surprised like that.

It was all her idea, I know. But she reminds me, anyway. The wife would not have done something like this. Not these days. These days her interests lie elsewhere, I'm afraid. I watch her as she goes out to the patio to smoke a cigarette and check her text messages.

—

Some mornings I kiss her while she sleeps and she is unaware. Doesn't she know I still love her? I have no right to be angered. Quietly, I rise from her side and go my own way before she wakes.

Rico said the people who lived in the walls were always complaining about the noise. It wasn't so much the rats as it was the family of Indonesian midgets living on the third floor, he said.

To call it a third floor was being generous. It was really just a part of the attic space over the eastern wing of the house that had been half-assedly converted to living space in the form of a ten-by-twenty room, one triangular vent that had been replaced with a triangular window, and no access except through a door that had been installed in the floor where the attic hatch had once been.

But the Indonesian midgets were a spry and hardy bunch, and they paid the rent on time, unlike the rats who stayed in a guest room at the opposite end of the house or the people who lived in the walls who had a penchant for going mysteriously silent whenever the landlord came around to collect the rent. All this was according to Rico, who told me everything about his living situation.

The rest of the house was occupied by Rico and his family. He said his father paid six-hundred per month for the rent, and that was a really good deal, according to Rico. I had no reference point to compare such a number, so it meant nothing to me. But I was happy for his father, nonetheless. I lived next door in my grandma's house there on Tulip Street and had no idea how much she was paying to live there.

Before Rico and his family moved in, the house had sat vacant for as long as I could remember. We weren't aware that anyone had bought the property until a crew of construction workers appeared one day with backhoes and sledgehammers and large metal dumpsters. They made quick work of that old house next door, which up until it was demolished, was an exact mirror image of my grandma's tiny little two-bedroom place with its one bathroom and cranky old faucet that made creaky groaning noises when you ran the tap in the morning.

We stood out on the porch one day watching a large backhoe dig into the front of the house, tearing away at the rotted wood and dilapidated siding. My grandma shook her head. "Ludwig and Irma Vanderweil lived in that house for sixty years," she said. "Ludwig passed in 1983. Irma stayed on for another -- ten years? They lived there a long time." She gurgled up a throatful of phlegm and hocked it across the porch.

I asked Grandma if she missed them.

"Oh, hell no!" she said. "They were freaks. Used to always see Ludwig going into that fag bar down the street. And I don't think Irma knew or even cared. What was it called? It's still there. Shit, I can't remember now. Oh wait....*The Roiling Stag.* You'd best avoid that place, son, if you don't want old men shoving fingers up your butt. That's what doctors are for." Grandma laughed, then she began wheezing, and went back inside.

Over dinner that evening -- fried baloney, chick peas, and buttered tortillas -- Grandma said, "I always thought that Irma was a witch, but I could never prove it for certain. Used to see her out in the backyard late at night doing stuff by herself. I wonder if they're going to find anything with all the digging they're doing out there."

If they did, me and Grandma never heard about it. The new house went up with little fanfare and a little grumbling from the neighbors, my grandma included. "Looks like a brick shithouse," she said. "An ugly brick shithouse." Then she went into a coughing fit and hocked a loogie across the lawn. I watched it fly like a greasy fat spider shot through a catapult.

She was right. The house was a two-story monstrosity. The thing towered over all the smaller and older homes on Tulip Street. It sat vacant for three years after construction was completed.

"Who'd want to live in it?" said Grandma, clearing her throat in a gurgling wheezing fit. "I can't believe someone would put so much money into a place to make it look like *that*."

I came home from school one day and found Rico bouncing a basketball in the driveway. I said, "Hello" and introduced myself. He regarded me with an amused yet murderous look and kept bouncing his ball. I stood there for a few moments, watching him, and as I turned to go inside, he said, "My name's Rico."

It was not his mother who had sent him outside to play with his basketball, he explained. His mother had passed away three years previous, run over by the very same bus that had faithfully delivered her to her job at the Haltom Inn where she worked as a housekeeper for ten years. Witnesses at the scene say they saw his mother throw herself in front of it. Rico scoffed, "Mi madre would never do that."

No, it was the people who lived in the walls who asked him to play with his ball outside. They were very sensitive about noise and had complained to the landlord. Rico's father told him he could no longer play inside the house or else they would be evicted. Rico pulled up his shirt and showed me the gashes and huge welts on his back. I could see scars beneath some of the fresher wounds.

"That's harsh," I said.

Rico shrugged. "My dad's always playing mind games like that. And sometimes in the middle of the night, the people in the walls come out to bite me."

At dinner that evening -- lamb chops and potato chips -- I told my grandma about Rico.

"That poor boy," she said, slurping the marrow from a lamb bone. "It's really tough growing up without a mother."

"But I don't have a mother," I said.

"Yeah, but you have me."

I forgot to tell her about the people who live in the walls or the wounds on Rico's back. Thinking back now, I probably should have.

Rico and I became best friends over the course of the school year. Maybe it was because we were only two of the six or seven Mexicans in the entire school; or maybe it was because we'd both lost our mothers; or maybe it was simply because we happened to be next-door neighbors. To this day, he was one of the best friends I ever had. I sometimes wonder how differently things would have turned out if we had remained friends through high school.

But perhaps such things were never meant to be, as my therapist would say to me years later.

Late one night my grandma and I were awakened by a commotion next door. We could hear glass breaking and shattering, people screaming, people crying, the thump-thump-thumping of something or someone being slammed against a wall. Before we could gather our senses to dial 911 or even make it out to the front yard to see what was going on, there came a quiet knocking on our front door. It was Rico. He was shivering violently and weeping.

"Please, can I stay here tonight?" he said.

"Does your father know you're here?" my grandma asked him.

His response was barely audible: "I don't know."

Grandma shooed him into the house then took a quick peek outside to see if anyone else was around, or watching. Silence. A lone lamp post down the street served only to illuminate a mist that had come in and hung low to the ground. Grandma shut the door and shot the deadbolts quick.

I made room for him on my bed, and as he undressed to get into my pajamas that Grandma had set out for him, I noticed splotches of blood on his underpants.

"Please, don't tell anyone," he sobbed. "Can I use one of yours? Just for tonight, please?"

I pointed to the bottom drawer, then turned to face the wall and went to sleep. It was a school night.

No one came looking for Rico the next day, and after school he went home just as if nothing had ever happened. I finished my homework and went out to the front yard hoping to see Rico out there bouncing his basketball just as he had done almost every day since I first met him, but I should have figured things would be different from here on out. Every window on Rico's house had been busted out from what I could see. Shards of glass and shattered pieces lay in the driveway and scattered across the lawn. Rico and his basketball were nowhere to be found. I was too afraid to go knocking on his front door to see if he was okay.

Over dinner -- sardines, rice, and a can of pork 'n beans -- I asked Grandma if we should call the police.

Grandma shook her head. "It's not our business, mijo," she said, picking the spine from a half piece of sardine with her fork. "It's not our business, and I'm way too old to be dealing with that kind of shit." She paused to cough into a napkin, then tossed it into the wastebasket.

We finished our dinner in silence, and while getting ready for bed, I remembered Rico's underpants. I searched through all the drawers, but they were nowhere to be found. Today was laundry day, I remembered.

I couldn't sleep that night, and evidently, neither could Grandma. I saw her bedroom light click on. I could hear her slippered feet shuffling into the living room. Then the sudden hum of the television being switched on -- SportsCenter. Re-aired, of course. ESPN anchors wouldn't be broadcasting live at two in the morning. I didn't know that at the time. I just took it for granted that sports were that important as it was to my grandma, the baseball fanatic. Go Yankees.

Rico didn't show up for school that next day, or the day after that. It was an uncomfortable time for me, forced to make new friends and hang out with new people, things I've never been very good at. I felt alone for a very long time after that, and in a way I blamed Rico for it.

One day I spotted one of the Indonesian midgets hammering a "For Sale" sign into the front yard of Rico's house.

"Where's Rico?" I asked the tiny man.

He stopped hammering and stared at me blankly. "I don't know who you're talking about, boy. Go home to your grandmother and pretend you never heard of him." He turned around and walked back into his house. Rico's house.

I shouted after him, "What about the people who live in the walls?"

49

I could see him peeking at me through the crack of the slowly closing front door.

Whether the house next door was ever sold or whether the family of Indonesian midgets and the people who lived in the walls were allowed to remain was a question that would remain unanswered. My grandma passed away shortly before Christmas and just after my eleventh birthday. Lung cancer. None of my relatives could be located, so I became a ward of the state and was made to live in a group home two hundred miles away until my eighteenth birthday.

It was years before I returned to that place where I once lived with my grandma. A dishonorable discharge from the Navy (for reasons I won't go into here) left me with a lot of free time to wander about the country and eventually find my way back to Tulip Street.

It had been nearly fifteen years, so long in fact that the street had been renamed to Market Way, and the block where my grandma's house once stood was now a parking lot for a busy strip mall complete with its own Super-Mart, theater multiplex, and two chain restaurants. If it wasn't for the railroad crossing and the gas station on the corner, I would not have been able to triangulate the approximate location of the spot where Grandma's house once stood.

I felt no sadness or sentimental feelings. I was amused, actually, at how quickly things had changed; how quickly those fifteen years had come and gone, as if my past had never existed, gone in a sudden flash. Maybe that was a good thing. I went into that Super-Mart to pick up some cold cuts and sandwich bread, and the cheapest bottle of red wine I could find. I was staying at the Super 6 Motel down the street and was hoping these supplies would last me at least for the next few days. The Navy never paid much, especially when you've been kicked out.

Remembering well my grandma's words of warning, and then completely disregarding them, I stopped by the *Roiling Stag* later that evening. It was still a gay bar by the looks of things. You could almost smell the semen and man-sweat oozing from the walls and feel the stickiness as you walked across the floor. I had just broken up with my girlfriend of five years. No real reason, I suppose -- I just didn't care anymore. Or for her, anyway. And now here I was, lurking about in the town's only gay bar. My triumphant return. Oh, well.

Echoing across the room, I hear a shrill voice singing over the Top 40 diva shit playing on the jukebox -- the intonations, the inflections, the barest hint of an accent -- the intervening years had added a slightly deeper resonance and masculinity to his voice, but I knew it was Rico.

From where I sat in the shadows at the end of the bar, I spied on him as he sashayed between groups of men sitting at the bar and near the pool tables. He wore a Catholic schoolgirl's outfit a la Britney Spears circa 1997. Lonely men sat eyeing him like animals in heat, barely able to contain themselves, fidgeting with excitement and making half-hearted, embarrassed attempts at groping Rico as he skipped by. He apparently knew how to play the game and played it very well.

I wondered, was it the people who lived in the walls that did this to him that years later would make a grown man parade around in a Catholic schoolgirl's outfit?

I left without saying a word or reintroducing myself. What was the point? Whatever lingering questions I had about life after Tulip Street no longer needed answering. The old street was gone, and that tired old facade had long since faded away.

The land out here is packed dense with scrub brush and small desert cacti. The property I own sits about a half-mile from a gravel road, and according to my GPS receiver, I was about fifteen-hundred feet away from the northeast corner. Wearing mud boots and armed with a ski pole I waded about a hundred yards deep before turning around and going back to the truck. I was paranoid about rattlesnakes and coyotes, and when I lost sight of the truck, I worried that I wouldn't be able to find my way back to it. I should have marked the place where I had parked as the starting point on my GPS receiver. It's real easy to lose your bearing and get lost amidst all that flatness. There are no physical landmarks. No hills, no mountains. Nothing. Scrub brush stretches out to the horizon, all around in every direction. It's like standing between two giant mirrors and experiencing that infinity effect.

No cell phone coverage, no electricity. The only water I had was the five one-gallon jugs stashed in the back of the truck.

I suddenly became aware of a stark reality: I could die out here and no one would know.

Nothing out there, out in the middle of nowhere.

As far as I could see, in every direction, miles and miles of sagebrush and desert flatness unfolded clear out to the horizon. A mere nine miles north of the town of Barstow, Texas, population 404, I knew then what it must feel like to be erased from life, Not dead, just erased. Moved to the nonexistent part of the universe, or parts of the American Southwest. If my truck broke down, it would be a long lonely walk back to I-20, and who knew what fate awaited me then? Murder, probably.

Parked along a dirt path just off the main gravel road, I unfolded a camp chair in the truck bed and sat for a while eating beef jerky and drinking from one of the gallon jugs of water that had been heated to what felt like 90 degrees from sitting in the baking sun.

I didn't notice at the time, but I had reached a milestone of sorts. That strange and wacky idea of living on uninhabitable "junk" land had come to fruition, at least partially. I wasn't really living out here just yet, just visiting. The thought of living this sort of lifestyle had become a philosophical and ideological obsession of mine after reading an article on SFGate.com about Phil Garlington's efforts at living on ten acres of desert land in far southern California that he'd purchased from a tax sale for three-hundred dollars. Little cartoon light bulbs went popping off all around my head. Who knew you could buy so much acreage for so cheap? Here we were struggling to pay the rent and pay my truck off. Whatever silly notions we had of buying a house in the Bay Area on my salary in 2003 were quietly, embarrassingly, put aside when we took a look at the local housing prices (over-priced, hyper-inflated) and figured out what our mortgage payment would be like if we tried to buy one of those overpriced pieces of shit (way too much). Come on, $500k for a 1,200 square foot 3-bedroom, 2-bath? Dumbfucks who just moved here from Third World countries snapped it up quick. "These houses are so affordable!" A year ago that same guy might have been squatting over a hole in the ground to take a shit. Suddenly banks are shoveling hundreds of thousands of dollars his way to go buy a house. Then these guys find themselves saddled with interest-only loans at 6.25% for 30 years. Six months later they are laid-off from high-tech jobs whose stock prices are no longer flying so high. Welcome to America, sucker! See you in foreclosure in a few years when that interest-only loan resets, assuming you and your new family can survive that long!

For us American-born slackers, single-family homes were out.

We worked our way down the list.

Townhouse? Nope.

Condo? Nope.

Mobile home? Nope.

Homeowners association fees. Lot rental fees. The cost for these were about what I used to pay for rent in San Francisco. Fucking crazy-ass skyrocketed prices. It's as if all the landlords in the Bay Area were conspiring to wring every last penny from all the desperate immigrants who were moving into the area, immigrants who had no sense of history of the place and had no idea of what prices were like even five years ago. "Fifteen-hundred for a one-bedroom shithole in East Palo Alto? No problem, sir! That's so wonderful! We will take it! That's a good deal! So much better than Mountain View or Sunnyvale!"

I was looking for the lowest common denominator. What was the cheapest shelter a person or family could live in and still manage to survive in the Bay Area?

I've heard of people living out of storage closets in the south of Market area in San Francisco. Further down a ways, on Third Street heading toward Candlestick Park, there are small groups of people living in old, beat-up trailers and vans parked along the side of the road. Most of these folks, I imagine, are getting by on subsistence checks and panhandling. If I could keep my lab-rat job, we'd be okay. But first we'd need a trailer and somewhere to park it.

I found just the sort of thing advertised on Craigslist. It was a trailer parked next to a house in Hayward with electrical and plumbing hookups. Asking rental price per month: $300. I called the guy, who had a strong Spanish accent, and asked if the trailer was still available.

"For you?" he asked.

"No, my wife and daughter, too. Three of us." I said.

He started laughing. "The three of you living in that trailer?"

"Uh, okay. Nevermind." I said and hung up. I could still hear him laughing as I clicked the "end call" button on my cell phone.

Sure, it sounds like a lunatic idea to choose to live like the borderline homeless and illegal immigrants in trailers and ramshackle tent-city encampments down by the river, all the while working a high-tech job and trying to raise a four-year-old, but as the saying goes, desperate times calls for desperate measures, and we were desperate as fuck. But I came around in the end. You can't raise a family like that, not unless your names are Meth-Head Dad and Crack-Ho Mom.

I use a spreadsheet to track our budget and was able to tell, month by month, how much money we should have in our bank account on any given day. The margins were slim. Actually...not so much slim as horribly anorexic. Two dollars leftover in May, and if we waited another four months, we might have another extra hundred bucks on which to splurge in September. Yay! Summertime fun.

Where was the money going? Rent, food, truck payment. In that order.

It was in this frame of mind, feeling the intense pressure of trying to raise a family in an over-priced housing market, all the while getting underpaid and under-sold, that I came across that article on Phil Garlington and off-grid living. I wasn't trying to save the environment. I was only trying to save ourselves. Nothing altruistic about it.

Phil Garlington and his ten acres spurred me on to discover other kinds of cheap shelter and forms of alternative housing -- converted school buses, shipping containers, yurts, tipis. There were tons of people already living the life, most of them refugees from the Summer of Love and looking like they hadn't bathed since around that time. Many were latter-day hippies -- kids born in the 80's and 90's whose outlook seemed to be a combination of 60's idealism and 90's angst with a dash of punk rock alienation, and sadly ending up with the worst from both worlds -- drug addicts riddled with venereal diseases and no real musical talent to speak of. But these are other stories to be told and have nothing to do with West Texas or my five acres of land.

Then there were the practical matters to consider -- recycling human waste via "humanure" compost bins, methods of generating one's own electricity, devising ways of harvesting water from the sky or sucking it out of the ground.

Each new thing to consider led me on to many new things to consider. If you're going to buy land out in the middle of nowhere, you'll need a clearing on which to set your shelter, and then you'll need roads in order to get to it. Gravel roads are fine. Dirt roads might be tricky. Four-wheel drive is highly recommended, especially one with high clearance, I soon discovered.

The land I bought is situated in the middle of a "subdivision" about half a mile from the main road, smack dab in the middle of dense underbrush and small cactus plants, exactly how it was described on eBay. EXCELLENT!! WOULD BUY FROM AGAIN!!! THANKS!!!!

I drove out there planning to camp out on my new property, but I didn't get farther than fifty yards from the dirt road before I started worrying about rattlesnakes, scorpions, and giant inch-long ants swarming out of holes in the flat hard ground. I'll have to come back with a good pair of snake boots and something to help clear some of that land, like a bulldozer or an army of Mexican day laborers armed with picks and shovels. It was painfully obvious that this wasn't something I'd be able to accomplish on my own. I can barely manage our tiny backyard space, which measures about 20-by-40, nevermind five acres of untended desert wilderness.

But still, I had achieved what I had set out to do three years earlier -- I had finally purchased my very own desert junk land out in the middle of nowhere, and as an added bonus, I somehow managed to buy a real house in a real neighborhood without having to pay a hyper-inflated asking price using an interest-only loan. It took our moving half-way across the country to North Texas to do all this, but we did it. It's surprising what a few years of constant obsession and scrambling and tooth-gnashing and hustling, hustling, hustling can accomplish. Gotta keep moving, gotta keep trying, more than that Nike ad campaign advising us to "just do it," just FUCKING do it.

I had actually purchased an acre of land in Havana, North Dakota a year earlier but have yet to travel out there to check it out. And any plans of actually living on this property or the one in West Texas quickly hit a wall of reality when Nadjet said to me, "What's

Sara's friends going to say when she invites them over to play with her in a shipping container in the middle of nowhere? Or what about her prom date? Don't you think she'll be embarrassed if he has to pick her up in a trailer in the middle of nowhere?"

She was right, of course. You can't raise a kid under those kinds of conditions unless you want them to grow up to be like that hill-dwelling freak from "The Hills Have Eyes."

It didn't really matter, anyway. We've got the normal house in a normal neighborhood now. The pressure isn't as intense as it was when we were scraping by in that rented apartment in California. It was this need to find affordable housing, which led me to discover alternative housing, and then cheap housing. I mean, you can't beat five acres of land for only $1,300, but you can't beat a 3-bedroom, 2-bath for $137,000, either.

Our three-year effort has yielded fruit. Now the real adventure begins.

—

Mexican guy pushing a bicycle along the shoulder of that West Texas highway off I-20, a long ways away from anything. Looked like all his worldly possessions were stored in the packs strapped to his bike. Dirty, dusty, sun-worn, tired looking and probably hungry. Cars and trucks sped by, myself included, leaving him in the dust, a shrinking spec in the rearview mirror. He might have been Buddha. He might have been Jesus. The poor Mexican guy with his bike on his way to perfection, long-suffering and patient. Why didn't I pull over and offer him a ride?

—

I pulled over at one of the rest stops to take a piss. I noticed a black kid sitting at one of the picnic benches. Couldn't have been more than eighteen or nineteen years old. He looked happy to see me when I pulled up. I got out and noticed an old beat-up Monte Carlo, or maybe it was a Cadillac, at the side of the road, one tire missing, the brake drum resting on the bare pavement. It was nearing dusk, and the sun's golden light was slowly sinking behind the horizon. Another half-hour or so and it would be night.

As I walked toward the restroom, the kid jumped up and came toward me. I nodded my head toward him in acknowledgment.

"I gotta pee!" he said. But the bathrooms were locked. I stood there chuckling and scratching my head while the kid walked around back to piss against the side of the building.

Then I hopped in the truck, started it up and sped off. Out of the corner of my eye I saw the kid running toward me, but I pretended not to see him and accelerated onto the highway.

Maybe he was going to rob me. Maybe he just needed a dollar. Maybe he just needed a ride into the next town or all the way into Dallas.

Point is, I didn't stop to offer any help when it was clear that the kid needed some.

All he had to do was ask. All I had to do was offer.

That was another test that I failed. I was fearful, untrusting, and selfishly worried that I would lose time getting home.

I didn't want to spend time cooped up with some babbling stranger in my tiny little truck. There's no room! Someone else will stop and give the kid a lift. Maybe the highway patrol who come by every few hours or so. I think.

I'm a selfish bastard. I'm a friggin' asshole. One day I will be all alone and in dire need of someone's assistance, and I'll have no one to blame but myself. I should have helped that kid. I knew I should have the minute I had merged back onto the highway. Why I didn't, I don't know.

Driving home Sunday afternoon after searching for lunch and not finding it, I head down Greenville Avenue in Richardson, my usual route home.

I pass through an "ethnic" business/restaurant part of town, a hole-in-the-wall area covering not more than two or three square blocks around where Belt Line Road turns into Main Street, comprising a small handful of Asian and Mediterranean places. I see the corner shop I always drive by and have always been meaning to visit but never have, until today. A Mediterranean cafe which sells ice cream, pizza, falafels, Coca-Cola, potato chips, and panini. I know this because each item is painted in large block letters on the front window.

The place is tiny and empty except for a man and his son. A sign near the narrow counter at the window reads: "Only people waiting for their food are allowed to sit here." (The ones trying to eat have to leave and find somewhere else to sit?)

I ask the guy behind the counter if he accepts American Express. He says, "You don't have Visa or Mastercard?"

"No," I say.

He stops to think for a moment. "Okay. I accept American Express. Would you like two large pizzas for only five dollars?"

"Um, no thanks," I say. I order the panini and take a seat at the counter near the window, where I am allowed to wait.

I notice the man taking a picture of his son, who is standing near the drink cooler holding up a bottle of Coca-Cola and smiling. Obviously tourists, I figure. Who else strikes silly poses with bottles of Coke in their hometown except for really bored people or teenagers?

"You guys want me to take your picture?" I ask.

"Sure, sure!" says the man. "These pictures are for my wife. She's out of town." He hands me the camera and motions for his son to stand next to him.

"Where's your wife?"

"Traveling on business." says the man, a little guarded. "In Tripoli, Libya." Then he smiles widely for the camera.

I snap the picture, then return to my seat at the counter. "I recognize the language you're speaking," I say. I ask him where he's from.

"Oklahoma," he says. From Libya originally, he tells me he's been living in Oklahoma for the last twenty-five years. A Muslim in Oklahoma? I'm tempted to ask him how he felt when that terrorist, Timothy McVeigh, bombed the FBI building in 1995, but stop myself. The irony might be lost.

Instead, I tell him my wife is from Algeria. His eyes light up. "Oh!" he says. "Do you read the Quran?"

"No," I say. (But I should have seen that question coming.) "The wife tells me it can only be read in Arabic, and since I don't speak the language...."

"No! That's not true," he says. Then, as if a door has been opened, he introduces himself and tells me his name is Nuredin Giayash. He tells his son to get something out of the car. The son returns shortly with a copy of the Quran. "Do you know what my name means? Your wife will know. You should tell her my name. It means 'searcher of the light.'" (Or something like that. I told the wife when I got home later that afternoon, and she just shrugged.)

Nuredin flips through the pages, finds the section he's looking for, and begins reading out loud. It's a chapter describing the Virgin Mary and the birth of Jesus. His son, standing just behind him, rolls his eyes at me. I get the feeling his father does this often -- reading chapters of the Quran to perfect strangers.

I understand the point he is trying to make. It's all interconnected -- the Bible, the Quran. Humanity. I'm guessing most Christians don't realize that the Muslim bible also tells the story of Jesus and the Virgin Mary's immaculate conception. It probably gets lost in all the other petty details that people would rather fight and argue pointlessly over.

It's all the same to me -- superstition and mythology. About as profound as believing in Santa Claus or the Easter Bunny. There is no way to prove that either exists, so why bother arguing one way or another?

The main teaching I take away from these various religions, the only commonality that I can find in Christianity, Buddhism, and Islam -- is that each prophet/hero/main character/protagonist -- Jesus, Buddha, Mohammed -- went out into the world on his own and made up his own mind about things. Each went off into the wilderness by themselves and met God on their own terms and through their own understanding. This is what we have to do, each of us, by ourselves. This much I believe and have come to realize. Everything else is mere story and anecdote to entertain the children and make it easier for the dumbfucks to understand.

And maybe this is the problem. Maybe organized religion is comprised of idiots and dumbfucks and people too afraid to go out on their own and make up their own minds about things and so stay huddled together? Strength in numbers. Strength in mob mentality.

I don't know. I'm not even sure that I've made up my own mind entirely. But I do know that I have no need to attend Sunday Mass and listen to some pedophile tell me what his interpretation of God is. I prefer to find out for myself.

I don't say these things to Nuredin. Instead, we exchange cell numbers by calling each other on our phones, promising to keep in touch. Why, I don't know. I'll probably never see him or his son again. Nuredin tells me that I can keep this copy of the Quran.

He starts to hand me the book, then pulls it back. "But one thing I must ask you, please," he says.

"What's that?"

"Do not set it on the floor."

"Okay."

"Do not read it on the toilet."

"Okay."

"Do you drink?"

"Uh....no?"

"Do not read it while you are drunk."

"Okay."

I thank him for the book and take my freshly prepared panini and head home.

Cancun: Day 1

Went through the security checkpoint at DFW International without being groped, harrassed, or otherwise sexually assaulted. The only hangup the TSA agent seemed to have was with my pair of Nike tennis shoes. He stopped the little X-ray machine, pulled aside the tray containing my shoes and called one of his supervisors over. They both poked and prodded my shoes for a few moments. Then she shrugged and gave the okay, and I was able to put my shoes back on. (Do my feet smell so bad that they set off their security scanners?

—

Eating croissants and drinking coffee just past the security checkpoint, Nadjet fishes through her bag and takes out her lighter. "Look," she says, holding it up. "They didn't even find my lighter. A lighter is a weapon!"

(STFU, woman!)

—

Pulled into Cancun at just past two in the afternoon. We were checked into our hotel and traipsing down Tulum Ave. in El Centro by 4:30. Making good time. The cab fare from the airport to the Radisson Hacienda downtown cost $600 pesos. Or $48.98US.

—

According to Google, the current exchange rate is: Mexican pesos divided by 12.27 equals US dollars. Pesos / 12.27 = US Dollars.

During our stay the exchange rate for the US dollar went as low as 11.40.

—

Cancun: Day 2

Judging by the run-down dilapidated state of many concrete buildings in Cancun's El Centro district, you'd think the city was built in the 1940s or 50s. Difficult to believe that this place didn't exist until 1974. (See notes from Day 4 below.)

—

Cracking up watching this old guy dive into a foot of water. Fooled by the foamy surf. He came up with a face full of sand and seaweed. Then a short while later, he did it again. He didn't learn the first time, apparently. Still fooled by the foamy surf. But he was smiling and laughing and enjoying himself nonetheless, splashing around in the surf with what appeared to be his grandson. The ocean has a way of turning all of us into fools and children. It's difficult trying to look calm and distinguished when the waves are slapping you around and knocking you over. You'll end up choking on a mouthful of seawater. Might as well laugh and play and enjoy it while you can.

—

Sitting on the hotel balcony, watching all the little taxis in the street below downshift into first gear as they creep over the speed bump. Brakes squealing, worn-out suspensions creaking and groaning. Bah-bump bah-bump...squee...squee...whirrrrrrrr!!

—

Another reason why netbooks are cooler than laptops: they're small enough to fit in the hotel room safe.

—

Little old Mexican lady across the bus station selling home-cooked tamales and tortas out of five-gallon buckets. A crowd of people gather around her each morning and wait patiently to place their orders. There are many such vendors around El Centro selling stuff out of five-gallon buckets every morning. They will situate themselves on busy corners where workers are lined up waiting to catch the little mini-van buses to wherever they need to go.

—

A small squadron of Mexican police stand guard outside a hotel entrance across from the ADO bus station. Many are very short, under 5'5", but size doesn't matter when you're dressed in riot gear and armed with AK-47s. They patrol the streets in packs of three or more, decked out in matching SWAT team blue jumpsuits, black combat boots, and helmets. And their AK-47s. Passing near them, I was always worried that one of them would accidently fire his rifle. "Oops! Lo siento!"

Later one afternoon, I see one of them without his helmet or AK-47, but still wearing his blue jumpsuit and boots, sitting on the curb waiting for a mini-van bus with all the other workers headed home for the day. Just another working stiff.

Oxxo stores are life-savers. Well, not really. But we stopped by almost every day to pick up our daily necessities: my large cup of coffee in the morning, cash from the ATM, six-pack of Dos Equis beer in the evening. Like their 24-hour convenience mart/gas station counterparts in the U.S., they're everywhere. We frequented the one down the street from our hotel near the Los Bisquets Bisquets diner on Avenue Nader. It's not as busy as the one across the street from the ADO bus station.

Also, there's a guy who parks his taco truck near there. I would usually see him pulling in and setting up his little motor-trike/taco truck thing just as I was leaving the Oxxo store with my cup of coffee, every morning seven o'clock on the nose. He would motor in with orange tent flaps fully extended, like some kind of mechanized flying nun. I was reluctant to try the food until the last two days of our trip. Those tacos were delicious! But something in one of those hot peppers caused an allergic reaction in me, and I suffered hives the entire week after our return.

Pro Tip: The ice bucket in the hotel room is barely large enough to hold ice and a single bottle of beer. Use one of the plastic trash bins instead. They are large enough to contain a twelve-pack of beer, plus all the ice you can dump into it from the ice machine down the hall.

Cancun: Day 3

El Centro's intersecting circular street patterns are dizzying and perplexing from the backseat of a tiny little taxi speeding around the roundabouts. Its design must have been based on the Mayan calendar.

Trying to navigate these streets on foot without a map is even worse. It's a circular maze of inner and outer loops. If you don't pay attention, you could be walking in circles for hours. I used the various Oxxo stores and hotel neon signs as markers to help me find my way, or at least tell me if I'm walking in circles. I was usually walking in circles. Lost and confused, I would still have to retrace my steps. I could have just hailed a taxi to take me back to the hotel, which would have cost about $20 pesos, but that would be cheating. The invading Spaniards didn't need taxis to help them find their way.

It's all gonna explode come December 21, 2012.

—

All was peace and quiet on the beach at Isla Mujeres until the chubby little girl started feeding Cheerios to the seagulls right behind our beach chairs. Little monster! (The girl, not the birds.) All the while her father sat there videotaping her, oblivious to the annoyance that the diving shit-bombs were causing other beachgoers. "Bad idea," I said, got up and dove back into the water. A bearded biker-looking old man, laughing and shaking his head, did the same.

—

Floating for hours along a Caribbean shore makes one lazier and even less inclined to do anything except crawl back onto the sand and take a long nap. Which is exactly what we did for three days in a row.

We've given up on the Hotel Zone completely, that wasteland of tourists and all the horrible things in the world that cater to such people -- the Hard Rock Cafes, the aggressive flea market proprietors, Vegas-styled nightclubs, douchebags and derelicts. Bleah. We now take the ferry out to Isla Mujeres, where the hotel operators encourage stragglers like us to use their beach chairs and umbrellas and offer us little white tables and menus for us to order from and eat on the beach. All for a price, of course. $200 pesos ($16US) per day to use their beach chairs. Free, if you order something from the menu. Not a bad deal.

Isla Mujeres is still touristy, but at least you don't have to worry about hotel proprietors chasing you off their lounge chairs.

I work with a guy who says he goes to Cancun every year with his family, but he has never heard of Isla Mujeres or Tulum. He's one of those vacation resort, all-inclusive types and never ventures beyond the hotel zone. Kinda sad.

—

Cancun: Day 4

Reached a milestone of sorts. Dropped my first load in a foreign public restroom. At the ADO bus station waiting for the 10:30 bus to Tulum, the stuff was ready to drop. $3 pesos took me through the turnstiles and into a relatively clean-looking, 1950's hospital-like environment. No puddles of urine on the floor, diarrhea-splattered toilet seats, or homeless-looking dudes loitering about suspiciously, like in American bus station restrooms. And unlike their American counterparts, each stall lacked its own toilet paper dispenser. A brief panic overcame me until I realized that there was a single toilet paper dispenser near the entrance. Just unroll what you need and take it with you into the stall. I went in with two fistfuls of the stuff and did my thing. Ahh....such a peaceful and relaxing experience.

Onward to Tulum.

—

I don't remember seeing so many tourists that last time we visited the Tulum ruins. This time they are everywhere.

Waiting for the tractor shuttle to take us 2,000 feet to the entrance to the Mayan ruins, the shuttle operators were charging $20 pesos a piece for the ride. We were each given a little green wristband to put around our wrists as proof of payment. It's a shakedown, like any other tourist activity here or anywhere else in the world where dumbfucks go to visit with sunscreen and loud American accents and plaid shorts and white tube socks with leather sandals. Funnier still are the old guys who arrive dressed in their best, most expensive explorer's outfits: safari hats, cargo shorts, and Columbia Sportswear button-down shirts. These dudes couldn't survive a day without air-conditioning or bottled water. And neither could I.

An old lady behind us wails, "Which arm are we supposed to put these wristbands on?"

"If you put it on your right," I say to no one in particular, "they'll carve your heart out at the end of the tour."

She doesn't laugh.

—

Cancun: Day 5

Breakfast alone this morning. The kid wants room service and the wife is hungover. She blames the cheap red wine.

"That wasn't wine," I say. "You drank the blood of the Sacrificial Tourist!"

"Go away," she says. "You're making it worse."

—

Generic aspirin and small bottle of hand sanitizer: $18 pesos ($1.46US). I ask the pharmacist if he sells codeine. He laughs and shakes his head, "No."

—

Huevos con chorizo y americano cafe: $73 pesos ($5.94US)

—

At the Royal Cancun, gardeners work to replace one type of grass (crab) with another (bermuda).

—

Walked from the hotel zone back to El Centro. In flip-flops. Long walk, long story, but the short of it is that the wife and I got into a bit of a tiff deciding which beach to plop ourselves down upon, so I turned around and said, "You know what? I think I'll walk back to the hotel." Or something like that. And I did. Two and a half hours and one blistered foot later, I was soaking in the hotel pool beneath clouds and cool weather.

The hotel shuttle bus dropped us off just beneath that Congo Bongo billboard, and I slowly made my way along Kukulcan, back out to Bonampak and up Avenue Nader to our hotel. Google Maps says it's only 5 miles, but that can't be right. Felt more like a ten-mile hike. I usually go for five-mile strolls around our neighborhood, and I have a pretty good idea how long it takes and how my legs and feet and knees feel. They were feeling like they do after trudging ten miles after that stroll back from the hotel zone.

Passed a few seemingly abandoned hotels along the way. Chain-link fencing wrapped around the perimeter. Vacant windows, empty buildings. Dead leaves and litter collecting in the corners. Near the entrance of one such place, I see a Mexican family coming down one of the pathways and remember that by law, these beaches along the hotel zone must remain open to the public. I venture down that same path and discover a beach that has been returned to its native state. Much of the powdery sand has washed away in places to reveal large toe-stumping rocks. There is no hotel groundskeeper to rake the seaweed, and it collects in huge swaths in the water and along the shoreline. The water is very shallow here, barely knee-deep out to a hundred yards or so. I see a young couple standing way out in the distance, quite a ways from shore. On the beach, a round Mexican woman sits with her baby on a blanket beneath a tree. I sit for a while after taking a quick dunk and enjoy the serenity and pristine quietness. Nothing like the Caribbean ocean to wash the sweat and soreness from one's body. Here there are no hawkers trying to sell me stuff or some tourist-filled restaurant blaring loud mariachi music across the beach. This stretch of property along Kukulcan, I later learn, is a man-made land bridge that connects what used to be a small island to the Cancun mainland. Cancun itself didn't exist before 1974 and developers wrangled it from the jungle when the Mexican tourism board wanted to find the "next" Acapulco. As the story goes, they entered all sorts of data into a computer and the computer spat out its result: Cancun.

—

Cancun: Day 6
The ATM machines dispense money in two-hundred-peso bills, but none of the street vendors ever have enough change to break it. So we're stuck with wads of two-hundred-peso bills in our pockets and no way to pay for any of that delicious food we see everyone eating.

—

3 beach chairs with umbrella for the day along the beach on Isla Mujeres, including 2 bottles of Dos Equis, 2 Cokes, 1 hamburger, 1 club sandwich: $215 pesos ($18US)

—

The wife has a thousand pesos and is betting ONE. PESO. AT. A. TIME. at the video slot machines. We're gonna be here FORfuckinEVER.

—

Cancun: Day 7
Hail, the Mayan sun!
And whores in brothels with their tired lingerie.
And the children running to school while the sun yet creeps over concrete cinder block buildings.

—

Bikini-clad blondes loading up on the scuba boat. Diver down! Diver down! Una mas, por favor!

—

3 lobster tails, 2 bottles of Dos Equis, chips and salsa: $340 pesos ($27US)

—

I find a fish carcass floating in the water. A seagull floats next to it, bobbing in the water and picking at its flesh. I pick it out of the water and bring it back to show the kid. As I was going to return it to the water, I pass an old guy sitting alone on his beach chair. "Hey! Where ya from?" he shouts. "Dallas, Texas!" I shout back. He joins me near the water with the fish still in my hand. Says he worked with Jacques Cousteau in the 70's, going on and on about filming some kind of shark episode with Cousteau not far from the island. Which is cool, except I'm holding a rotting fish carcass in my hands and want to throw it back in the water.

—

Cancun: Day 8
U.S. traffic patterns: me me me me STOP!! you you you you STOP!!
Mexican traffic patterns: me you me you weave drift you me me slow down bump me you me me you you

One of Plano's finest pulled me over just as I was about to merge onto the freeway on my way to Dallas for some Mexican food Friday night.

Probably got me for speeding, I thought, pulling into the U-Haul parking lot. But no. He says he pulled me over for failing to signal a lane change. Okay, fair enough.

He asks for my driver's license and proof of insurance then walks back to his squad car. He returns a few minutes later. "What'd you get arrested for in California?"

"Uh...what year?" I say.

"It doesn't give a year. It just says you were arrested," he says. "You don't remember what you were arrested for? Most people would remember."

"Well, I haven't lived there in years. What incident are you referring to? I've been arrested a number of times."

"Where ya headed?" he asks.

"Dallas."

"Why you going to Dallas?"

"What, I can't go to Dallas? I'm gonna get something to eat."

"You're going all the way to Dallas to get something to eat?" he says. "What restaurant you going to?"

I mumble random Mexican-sounding restaurant names. "La Panchillo...La Paisano...La Bamba. Ahh, I can't remember."

"You can't remember the name of the restaurant you're going to?"

"It's a hole-in-the-wall place, but I go there all the time."

"You go there all the time, but you don't know the name of the place?" he says. "You're going all the way into Dallas on a Friday night to have dinner by yourself?"

I shrug. "My wife doesn't like to go."

"So you're leaving your wife at home to go eat dinner by yourself? That doesn't make sense." He smirks. "You going to visit your girlfriend?"

"No," I say. And even if I did, what fucking business of it is his? I'm getting annoyed that this cop is jumping all over my back asking idiotic questions. I'm about to tell this dude to go fuck himself, but I try to remain calm. He's younger than me by about fifteen or twenty years, and I'm getting too old for this shit. I have a mortgage and a family, and I'm thinking now that I should have just stayed home.

"Do you have anything in the truck that I should know about? Guns? Drugs?"

"No."

"Would you mind if I searched your vehicle?"

"Go right ahead."

He pulls me out of my truck there in the U-Haul parking lot just off the service road along I-75. He pats me down, and then we wait for his backup to arrive.

I'm at a point in my life -- and I believe most people arrive at this point sooner or later in their own lives -- where I feel absolutely no need to make small-talk with anyone for any reason. Better to simply remain quiet.

But we start chatting, anyway. He tells me my inspection sticker is expired. "Shit, I always forget to check that."

"Most people do," he says. "Also your right tail light is out. You might want to get that fixed before you get it inspected. You can get a ticket for those."

I say nothing and change the subject. I ask him how long he's been working out here. "Five years!" he says. He says he's from Kentucky originally, and suddenly his thinly-veiled hostility and accusatory questioning from the outset starts to make sense. I'm not white and I'm dressed like a bum, so I must be guilty of something.

I ask him how he likes it out here. "I LOVE it out here!" he says excitedly.

He tells me they're searching vehicles along the freeway because there have been a lot of guns going into Dallas from Plano. Which makes no sense to me. In fact, it sounds pretty fucking retarded. How does one search vehicles along the freeway? Randomly? Stop every fifth one? Stop only the drivers who look Mexican or black?

"Huh," I say.

"What year's your truck?" he says.

"2003."

"How many miles?"

"One-sixty-one."

"I got a 2004. Hundred-twenty-five on it."

"I've driven this thing out to West Texas twice," I say. "Blew out a few tires just outside of Pecos the first trip. The sidewalls just started bubbling up. Blew out the engine on the second trip."

"Did you try any Pecos cantaloupes?"

"What's that?"

"Pecos cantaloupes. They're known for their cantaloupes," he says.

"I didn't know that," I say. "I was heading out there to check out some land I bought on eBay."

"How much you pay for it?"

"Just over a grand."

"Not bad. Does your land have cantaloupes on it?" he asks.

I start laughing. "I recently bought some land out in Sulphur Springs. It's got electricity, water, septic."

"My parents own some land out near Paris," he says.

"How much acreage?"

"Couple hundred acres."

"Damn."

"There's a lotta meth labs out there," he says.

"Really? I've heard it's really bad in Oregon. Didn't know they had that problem out here."

"It's real bad," he says.

His backup arrives after fifteen minutes or so. My new friend takes a few minutes to search my truck while I wait leaning against the bumper of his squad car. He returns and hands me my driver's license back.

"Enjoy your dinner," he says. "Sorry to take up so much of your time."

"No problem," I say.

I hop into the truck and drive into Dallas for some Mexican food. He didn't ticket me for the expired inspection sticker or the broken tail light.

I notice the buzzing while eating a plate of beef enchiladas. Seated at my usual spot in a booth near the window, I glance over and see a fly upon the windowsill resting on its back, sporadically buzzing like a miniscule alarm clock. First buzzing and spinning clockwise. Now buzzing and spinning counterclockwise. The little guy is obviously in some sort of distress. Is he injured? I look closer. All of his legs appear to be moving and kicking about. Perhaps he'd been poisoned. I am seated in a restaurant, after all, the sort of establishment that doesn't take kindly to his kind.

I slurp another forkful of melted cheese and cut another section from my enchilada. Meanwhile, a tiny creature just to my right upon the windowsill suffers the pangs of death and prepares to pass to the other side. Is the pain the same -- passing from this life to the next -- for every living thing regardless of size, intellect, or higher consciousness? This tiny fly struggles to live, even now as it takes its last gasps of life. It will not go quietly into the night. I swill my Corona and slurp down another forkful of melted cheese and beef enchilada.

Who's to say if one creature's suffering is more or less worthy than another's? Or more or less deserving of compassion and sympathy? For long minutes, I observe the fly writhing upon the windowsill. Its suffering is genuine. This is not merely dramatics. The fly knows nothing of the protocol of death. It is simply dying. And yet the will to live is strong and so it fights on, this little fly upon the windowsill.

I bear witness to a phenomenon so seemingly natural and obvious that it almost goes without saying -- everything living must one day die -- and yet its occurrence seems so abhorrently unnatural when seen firsthand, this passing from one state of existence to some unknown other. Before me, the fly is preparing for such a journey. Such meaning could not have been appreciated if I had simply swatted it out of its misery with a rolled up newspaper or flicked it away with a finger with no further thought about it. It is a different spectacle to sit and watch the life slowly slipping away of its own accord, this miracle of life passing slowly before your eyes. Indeed it is a mystery. It is too easy to kill things, too easy to be a force of destruction. If we had the merest inkling of what it takes to breathe life into a thing, we would have a deeper understanding of its preciousness, even something as seemingly insignificant as this fly, whose buzzing is slowly tapering off, the moments growing longer between each wing flutter, until at last it comes to a stop. Eternal stillness.

I finish my meal and order another Corona. My waitress with her flashing smile stands close and tells me there is dancing here, and live music too, on weekend nights from nine till closing. Maybe I'll stop by, I say to her.

Farewell, little fly. In the course of a lunchtime meal on a lazy Saturday afternoon, you endured what those of us still living have yet to experience. You were not the ruler of kingdoms. You did not change the course of world events. You were not famous, nor did any come to seek you out. You were just another stupid little fly living and dying upon a windowsill. Does it make your passing any less significant? Every life a spark from a fire. A momentary flash of something beautiful and infinitely mysterious.

I get up to pay the cashier, wondering if I will have the same strength and resolve to survive when it comes my turn to die.

Cabo San Lucas looks a lot like West Texas, except with beaches and strip clubs. Our visit, unfortunately, coincided with peak tourist season -- drunk white kids everywhere.

The beaches are scenic, perfect for taking honeymoon photographs, but there was only one we found that was actually swimmable -- along the far western end of Medano Beach, going towards the docks. This annoyed my wife considerably and soured what would have otherwise been an enjoyable vacation.

Also, we got a little carried away with the spending, but what can you expect when you take back-to-back trips to San Francisco and Cabo? We went way overboard and rang up $5,000 on one of our credit cards, which is something we've never done and certainly not for any single vacation or two. We've always tried to pay cash for such expenditures. What makes the sting of debt even more acute is that we didn't really enjoy ourselves in Cabo. In fact, this was probably one of the worst vacations we'd taken in a while, second only to that week-long trip we took to South Beach, Miami in 2004. Obviously, any vacation, no matter how long, beats staying at home doing nothing, but the time and money we spent in Cabo probably wasn't worth all the fussing, fighting, and arguing we did while we were there.

If you're a diehard beach-goer like my wife, whose sole purpose for taking any vacation is to lie out in the sun and then, after being sufficiently warmed, going for a dip into nice, calm, warm, and shallow ocean waters, you might want to rethink Cabo. Nice, calm, warm, shallow -- the water along Cabo's beaches are none of these things. The guide books are right, and I should have taken heed. That was my fault. I booked the trip before doing any kind of research. Then I opened up a copy of "The Complete Idiot's Travel Guide to: Mexico's Beach Resorts" and discovered this entry for Cabo: "The lodgings in San Jose's hotel zone line up along Playa Hotelera, a wide and lovely stretch of sand lapped by water that's, sadly, subject to a strong undertow, rendering it unsafe for swimming."

That's a clinical, understated way to put it. The reality is you've got five- to six-foot waves breaking on the shore, literally pounding sand with each set that rolls in, and when the water goes rolling back, the undertow is powerful enough to pull you off your feet and suck you under. It can be a painful (and life-threatening) experience to be caught in the middle of all this wave-breaking and sand-pounding. None of us being very good swimmers, we stayed away from these places, which unfortunately, was true for most of Cabo's beaches.

Nadjet was miserable those first few days, and we were only going to be there a week. To make things worse, a hurricane had blown through the day before we arrived, which made for ice-cold water along the shores. It was like swimming in the waters off northern California -- cold, cold, cold. So not only were the beaches unswimmable, even if you did find a place that was safe to swim, the water was ice cold. I tried braving it, anyway, but couldn't last for more than a few minutes before my fingers and toes began to go numb. Way too cold.

The beach situation didn't bother me, really. I was content to go exploring the town. I had warned Nadjet we might not find any good beaches. In fact, I had shown her that little blurb in "The Complete Idiot's Guide." It was too late. The trip had been booked and now here we were. If we couldn't go swimming, I figured we could at least enjoy the scenery, but even then there wasn't much to see. At least to the untrained eye. Baja California is a dry, dusty desert environment. The barren landscape, dotted here and there by cactus plants and scrub brush, runs right out to the ocean. There is no gentle transition of landscape, no subtle change of scenery. The contrast is as direct as the burning sun at high noon. Here, it is all or nothing -- the desert or the beach.

There was one other option, one other place where we could hang out and explore. This place is always the same no matter where it is, and you will never fail to encounter the same kind of crap and the same kind of people. It could be Front Street in Lahaina, Kuhio Avenue in Waikiki, Lincoln Road in South Beach, Fisherman's Wharf in San Francisco, or the tail end of Mexico's Highway 1 in Cabo San Lucas -- the tourist zone, a lifeblood for locals and scorned by travelers and vagabonds who consider themselves more sophisticated than the average "tourist." The t-shirts and shot glasses might bear the name of various cities imprinted upon them, but chances are they are all made in the same tourist tchotchke factory somewhere in the middle of China, where the workers are forced to churn out that crap in such high volume that they rarely have time to see their families, much less have time to take them on vacations to those very same places where those t-shirts and shot glasses are destined.

In Cabo San Lucas, the tourist shops and restaurants are strung along the tail end of Mexico's Highway 1 as it turns into the city street, Lazaro Cardenas. There is a little downtown area and the road appears to run smack into a large mountain, the other side of which lay the Pacific Ocean.

Many of the tourists have that southern California look -- blonde-haired and sun-tanned, clean-cut and extroverted, prowling Cabo's narrow city streets in packs of five or more. Like the Chinese or Japanese, it is very rare to find one traveling alone.

We didn't travel all that way to stare at tourists all day. Our place at the Santa Fe Hotel was far enough from the tourist zone that it never became an issue. There was one other American couple there, a portly older couple in their fifties or sixties who spent most of their time lounging in the pool area. They were at the pool every day -- when we left in the morning and when we returned in the afternoon, there they were -- hanging out poolside.

The Santa Fe is more of a locals-only place -- laid back, understated. There were no tequila parties and sunglassed DJs at the mic blaring club music with drunken coeds parading around the courtyard. Many of the guests appeared to be Mexican, businessmen perhaps, visiting from Mexico's other states.

The rooms were strange. The entrance to each was through a sliding glass patio door, just like the ones you see in suburban houses leading out to the backyard. At check-in, I asked the clerk if he could give us a second key for Nadjet to use. He shook his head, no. There was only one key per room.

The hotel was constructed in a U-shape, with each sliding glass door facing inward toward the pool area, sort of like a motor court apartment complex. As we made our way up to our room on the second floor, which was directly over the pool area, we watched a number of men sitting at the patio tables quietly watching us back. They didn't look like tourists or vacationers. I had visions of them chainsawing someone's leg in one of the rooms. The fact that the entrance to our room was through a sliding glass door and only locked with a latch with no deadbolt didn't make us feel any safer. Maybe it was the American in us that made us feel so concerned about safety and security. The other guests seemed not to mind.

The air-conditioner wasn't working despite pressing random buttons along the front panel. Same deal with the TV and the mini-fridge. Neither seemed to be working -- no matter how hard I clicked that TV remote control or how many times I opened and shut the door to that mini-fridge. Whatever. We could do without those, but we definitely needed to get that air-conditioner working. No way we'd be able to sleep in that 95F- to 100F-degree heat. Within ten minutes of checking in, we were about ready to check-out. Feeling a little guilty that I might have checked us into a flea-bagged shit-hole for the next seven days, I suggested to Nadjet that maybe we could see about finding another hotel the next day.

I walked back to the front desk and told the clerk about the air-conditioner.

"The buttons aren't working," I said.

"Buttons?"

"Yes, the buttons along the front. I push them and nothing happens."

"Did you try the remote control?"

"Remote control?"

"Yes, it's controlled by the remote. It is all explained on the instruction card in your room."

"Oh. And the TV's not turning on, either."

"The TV and the refrigerator are unplugged. You have to go under the cabinet and plug them in. That is also explained on the instruction card, which is in your room."

I made a mental note for next time -- RTFIC: "Read the fucking instruction card."

Having been gently reminded of my incompetence and thusly humbled, I shoot back up to the room and discover everything works precisely as the front desk clerk (and that instruction card) advised.

The place grew on us after the first few days. It remained quiet and low-key for the duration of our stay. The beds were firm. The toilet flushed. The water pressure in the shower was nice and strong. The air-conditioner, once I figured it out, hummed along quietly, keeping everything nice and cool.

As had become habit now, whenever we go on vacation, each morning while Nadjet and Sara are still asleep, I'll slip out and go for an early morning stroll through the city. In the morning, in June in Cabo, temperatures were still cool enough to go rambling about town on foot in the crisp cool early morning ocean air. As the hour approached noon, the temperature would shoot up to around ninety degrees and last until sunset, when the temperature would again drop down to seventy as a cool evening breeze blew in from the ocean. Having spent the past five years in Texas, it was refreshing to again experience the cooling effects of living in a coastal town. Texas has the shittiest weather, and so any place looks better in comparison. If you can live in Texas, you can live anywhere.

I found a cafe a few blocks away. This would become my go-to spot every morning. The coffee was strong, the bagels were fresh, and as near as I could tell, it was the only place open within a ten-block radius. This town is a bit more laid-back than Cancun, where working-class Mexicans could be seen crowding bus stops on almost every corner each morning. Mornings in Cabo found only a few souls wandering about. Very few places, I learned, opened before 9AM.

One exception was the Mexican woman who worked the breakfast/lunch counter at our hotel. Each morning as I left for my walk, I could see her through the counter window, prepping everything and getting ready for the breakfast "rush" -- two or three guests. The wife and kid would still be asleep when I returned, so I would sit downstairs and order breakfast.

The woman would smile and sort of give me a sideways look the first few times I ordered breakfast from her. Then one day she asked me (in broken English) if I was a famous pianist. She said some name, which I no longer recall, then she pretended to play an invisible piano and pointed at me. I shook my head and laughed. No, sorry. Just another slouch from the States. The breakfast there was a little pricey by Mexican standards -- $7US for a bacon omelette with the works. In fact, Cabo in general was more expensive than Cancun. Except for the rental car, for some reason.

At my cousin's suggestion, who visits Cabo every year, we rented a car at the airport for $4 per day. After taxes and insurance, it came closer to $24 per day. Still a bargain which ended up costing us around $200 for the entire week. Not bad. That little Renault Rio was fun as hell to drive around El Centro's narrow streets, scooting past buses and weaving through crowds of pedestrians. I kept remarking to the wife that if they sold those back in the States, I would definitely look into buying one. It's perfect for running errands around town. Probably wouldn't recommend it for people who are over six-feet tall or weigh more than two hundred pounds. It'd be kind of a tight fit.

It was a good thing we rented that car. Nadjet's obsessive need to find the perfect beach had us driving all up and down the coastline. It was like going to the beach with Goldilocks -- everywhere we went, the water was either too rough or too cold. We argued and fought the first few days because of this. Nadjet was upset she couldn't find that one perfect beach, and I was angered and annoyed that she couldn't just enjoy the place for what it was. The tourist zone disgusted her, especially, and Cabo San Lucas is all tourist zone. Each evening, she retired to the hotel room and declined my invitations to go walking around and exploring the neighborhood. It's too hot. She's too tired. There is nothing to see except drunken tourists in overpriced gift shops. She may have been right, but I refused to let that stop me from checking out all the sights. This was still a strange and alien town to us, after all, despite the Hardrock Cafe and Sammy Hagar's "Cabo Wabo." These streets I had not wandered before. These people I have never seen in my life.

Downtown Cabo is a tiny place, barely encompassing a two- or three-mile area. It didn't take long to figure out the boundaries of the various neighborhoods -- tourist zone to the southeast along the waterfront and the residential area to the north. The locals seemed more well-off than the locals we saw in Cancun. In Cabo, the bus stops aren't crowded and many seem to drive their own cars. They don't seem as friendly, either. Many seemed to possess a blank smile, a thin facade beneath which you could just barely detect a secret contempt and disdain they might have felt toward the blonde-haired tourists who have overrun their home and to whom they have become so dependent upon for their livelihoods. Or maybe it's just me reading too much into it.

I sympathized with these people -- the poor ones, the ones who have to work the lunch counters; the ones who have to clean hotel rooms; the ones who are forced to sell trinkets on the beach, constantly pestering you with their wares while you try to enjoy the sound of the waves and the ocean breeze. At first, you politely decline their wares and services. "No, thanks." "No, gracias." But they persist. "Lo siento. No mas dinero." And finally you just start to ignore them, look the other way, pretend you don't see them as they drift on by, like ghosts.

These people have no choice -- living in a tourist town, there is very little industry except tourism. They are dependent on the money that tourists bring into their little area of the world. Seems like a fragile existence to me, being dependent upon the well-being of foreigners and made to live like scavengers and parasites. Maybe some don't care. Perhaps some never come to realize it. If the tourists go away, what happens to the locals?

It was cold out there on the water and getting colder as the sun drifted down toward the horizon. We didn't think to bring extra sweaters or blankets, as some of the other more well-prepared passengers had done. We were on a "pirate" cruise ship sailing around the southernmost tip of Baja California. I assumed most if not all of the passengers scored their tickets like we did -- by enduring a three-hour timeshare seminar. Or actually, what the wife and kid had to endure; I spent the morning on the beach. Nadjet received the invite from the owner of our hotel, a fast talking guy, young, well-dressed and successful looking with his slicked back hair, starched collar, gold rings, and expensive-looking watch. I wondered, how much of a kick-back does he receive for referring his hotel guests to these timeshare seminars?

Nadjet was sold on the pirate cruise and the free breakfast. I tried to remind her about the last time we got stuck in a timeshare seminar, but she was too excited about the idea -- "Pirate cruise ship! Free breakfast!" -- and maybe for her it was a welcome distraction from her ongoing disappointment regarding the beach situation. I had fears of some local drug cartel kidnapping timeshare attendees and selling them into slavery. Or worse -- enduring a three-hour hard-sell by wide-eyed cult-like timeshare sales people and then later being stuck on a crowded "pirate" ship with a bunch of bloated tourists yapping and snapping pictures. This wouldn't be far from the truth. Anything involving tourists or timeshares or "free" cruises -- you count me out. I'd rather eat stale sandwiches sitting on dusty curbs while watching the locals go about their daily routines. This other stuff geared toward tourists and their money strikes me as Disneyland fakery and fills me with the urge to defecate. No, thanks.

—

Just as the host of our pirate cruise ship had predicted, the wind picked up considerably as we sailed around the southern tip of Baja California and into the choppy waters of the Pacific Ocean. Whoever thought it was a good idea serving free alcohol to a bunch of landlubbers and then taking them for a ride through rough, choppy waters either failed to account for the seasickness factor or took secret pleasures in watching tourists barfing everywhere. An attractive young woman -- looking respectable and proper with her newly-acquired husband -- sat discreetly behind the open bar pretending to enjoy the view. Every once in a while she'd lean forward and projectile vomit a mouthful of green sludge into a large garbage can next to her. She'd take a napkin, dab her chin and cleavage with it, and go back to enjoying the view.

The free dinner was a buffet style serving of taquitos, tortilla chips, Mexican fried rice, refried beans, guacamole, salsa sauce, and sour cream. Mexican food as interpreted by American chain restaurants and toned down to suit blander American palates. We piled the stuff onto flimsy paper plates and sat down to eat amidst whipping winds periodically spraying us with ocean water.

A few crew members began climbing around a rope tied high up on the rigging. One guy held on to the rope while another guy pulled him back and swung him over the edge of the ship and out across the water. He swings back and lands on the platform. Ta-da. A few people clapped. Then he did it once more. Ta-da.

The emcee asks over the mic if any guests want to take a swing on the rope.

Huh? This makes no sense. Seems too risky. Why would a tour company allow people to swing on a rope, without a life jacket, over open water? The water is cold and choppy. The wind is howling while the ship rocks heavily from side to side. Then I remember we are in Mexico, where laws and regulations are either lax or non-existent. Regulations? We don't need no stinking regulations!

A middle-aged guy raises his hand. He's there with his two young children and beautiful blonde wife who's dressed as if she's attending the Kentucky Derby -- summer dress, parasol hat and all. He gulps down one last spoonful of refried beans and steps up to the platform. He wraps the end of the rope around his wrist and holds on tight as one of the crew members pulls him back and swings him out over the water. No life jacket, swinging across cold choppy water in the open ocean. He doesn't lose his grip and lands safely back on the platform.

Ta-da.

People clap. The emcee asks if anyone else wants to try. A teenaged girl raises her hand.

"And how old are you, senorita?" he asks her. Fifteen, says the girl. "Is it okay, Dad?" The girl's dad nods his approval.

The girl grabs hold of the rope, swings out over the water, and lands safely back on the platform. Ta-da.

Then the girl's little sister wants to give it a try. Repeats the feat. No big deal. Ta-da.

It's growing colder as the sun drifts down toward the horizon. All I can think about is getting back to land and our hotel. This is the last fucking time I'm letting myself get talked into going on a "sunset pirate cruise."

The emcee announces the next event, which involves calling various women up to the stage and asking them to perform idiotic parlor tricks or some such crap, but before he can continue, someone in the audience raises a hand.

"Oh, wait!" says the emcee. "We have another volunteer to swing on the rope!"

A young Mexican woman wants to have a turn. She hurriedly hands her plate of rice and beans to her companion, almost dumping it into his lap, then she gets into position on the wooden platform. A crew member hands her the rope, and she grabs it at the tip. Her hands are resting just above the large knot tied at the end. Two crew members pull her back then shove her out over the edge of the ship. She swings around in a wide arc. The water is cold and choppy. It is extremely windy out here along the southern tip of Baja California, and it becomes apparent that this young woman has never swung on a rope in her life. Her legs are kicking in every direction, and she's gripping the rope at the very end. As she swings back she comes in way too low and hits the water up to her waist. For some reason -- probably out of panic or from the shock of cold water -- she lets go of the rope. She begins dog-paddling alongside the ship, but we're moving at a fast clip and starting to leave her behind.

"Save her!" I yell.

The crew members look confused and a little surprised that someone actually fell into the water. The girl's boyfriend or fiance looks equally dumbfounded. He just stares at her down there in the water. From where I'm sitting, I can see the girl's eyes wide with fear as she paddles desperately.

Someone suddenly remembers that there's a life-preserver designed specifically for this sort of occasion. The crew members dig around for it....it's got to be around here somewhere. The normally chatty, wise-cracking emcee has gone silent. He's as shocked as the rest of us. They find the life-preserver tucked under a bench and hurl it over the side in the general vicinity of where the girl is dog-paddling. One of the guys dives in after it, like a true pirate. When they finally get her aboard, she is soaked. She had been wearing jeans and a frilly white blouse, and now she just looks like a wet cat. She spends the remainder of the trip below deck in the cabin wrapped in a blanket.

The temperature continues to drop as the wind picks up. We seem to be floating endlessly. The emceee has run out of stupid games to play, so they turn up the music. AC/DC's "Highway to Hell" blares from the loudspeakers. Fitting music for a sunset dinner cruise on a pirate ship in Mexico. The ship wheels around and everyone takes out their cameras -- there it is: Sunset over Cabo San Lucas.

Cabo's version of Skid Row is a broken down street on the northeastern part of town that stretches for three blocks north to south and is lined by whores, drunkards, and hole-in-the-wall dives. On any other day this would have been my preferred hang out, but with my new friend, Pablo, acting as captor and chaperone, I'm not really feeling that adventurous vibe. I just want to go back to the hotel, shower, and take a nap. Crawling around the shitty part of town with this Ultimate Fighter has-been is wearing me down.

But I'm getting ahead of myself.

Every tourist town has them -- hawkers and fixers and two-bit hustlers. Men -- they're usually men -- living off the scraps of tourists. They spend their lives out there on busy sidewalks and street corners handing out flyers, coupons, offering their services to show you around their beautiful city. They say they will bring you to all the popular bars and restaurants -- or for the guys who appear to be traveling alone -- strip clubs and whorehouses. Cabo is no exception.

The trick to dealing with these guys is to just ignore them and keep walking. The moment you stop to engage them in any kind of conversation is the moment they think they've got a sale. Your slightest acknowledgment is their cue to move in and bombard you with the sales pitch. Timeshare presentations. Dinner at a new restaurant. Dinner at an old restaurant that's under new management. Discount tour packages. Glass-bottom boat tours. Swimming with dolphins. Whatever. It's all bullshit you don't need, but they'll try to sell it to you anyway.

I was walking back from the little Main Street shopping area that runs along the waterfront heading north into the more rundown part of town where the locals live and where our hotel was located, and as I'm crossing the street, crowds of Mexicans around me, a tall muscular guy approaches from the opposite direction. He's holding his arms out wide and smiling right at me, "Hola!"

I move to step around him, thinking his greeting is directed at someone behind me, but no -- he angles straight for me and grabs me by the shoulder and shakes my hand. His hand is rough and calloused, like one who spends his time performing manual labor. Or pounding tourists into bloody pulps. There is a scar running down the entire left side of his pock-marked face, which bears additional scrapes and scratches. His nose is slightly crooked, like it had been broken more than a few times.

He greets me in Spanish and says a few other things that I don't understand. I try to wave him off, "Lo siento, no habla Espanol."

"Oh, you speak English!" he says, walking alongside me. His eyes narrow. "I don't believe you don't speak Spanish. Where you from?"

"Texas," I say.

"No, I mean what's your nationality?"

"My parents are from Hawaii." I tell him. I'm walking faster now, trying to put some distance between us, but he's keeping pace.

He suddenly becomes excited and animated. "Oh, man! Do you know Kimo? I used to train with him, man!"

I tell him I don't know who Kimo is.

He looks at me sideways. "How can you call yourself a Hawaiian if you don't know who Kimo is?"

I shrug.

"He was one of the greatest Ultimate fighters of all time! Oh man, you can't be a true Hawaiian if you don't know who Kimo is! You know, when he used to go into the ring, he would carry a big wooden cross. And he had a tattoo of angel wings on his back."

We've walked two blocks now and he's still following me. He hasn't yet given me his sales pitch, but I know one is coming. Or maybe he's just planning to rob me? He seems crazy and desperate enough.

He narrows his eyes again. "Hey. Hey, man. What you looking for?"

"Nothing," I say.

"What you want? You wanna go to a club? You wanna see some girls? Hey, lemme show you around." He's standing very close, leaning into me, invading my personal space. I'm shaking my head, telling him no, no, no. He either doesn't get that I don't want to be bothered or he doesn't care.

I catch a glimpse of his hands -- knuckles gnarled and scraped with what appear to be fresh cuts upon them. These could very well be the hands of a man who had just pounded someone into the pavement. It makes me think twice about just telling him to fuck off and leave me alone.

I feel trapped as he steers me into a hole-in-the-wall grocery store. It seems the owner recognizes my new friend and shoots him a contemptuous glare. He watches suspiciously as we make our way to the back of the store where we find various meats, dried fruit, and other items stored in large plastic bins.

Pablo helps himself to a handful of peanuts. "See these? Try some. They're delicious."

I glance over my shoulder and see the owner still watching us.

"Oh, here," says Pablo, reaching into a bin of freshly baked potato skins. "Go ahead, try some. This shit is really good."

When he's had his fill, we leave without paying. We're nearing our hotel, and I don't want him to know where we're staying. I tell him I have to get going.

"Where?" His eyes narrow. "Where you staying?"

I lie and tell him we're staying at one of the hotels along the waterfront.

"Then why you walking this way?" he says accusingly, correctly pointing out that we're headed in the wrong direction. "You don't even know where you're going! You're lost!" He laughs and slaps me on the back. "C'mon, let's go get a drink. I know this place around the corner."

The wife and kid are back at the hotel, probably where I am right about now. Scared? Frightened and intimidated? Not wanting to get the shit kicked outta me on a strange street in a foreign land for a measly two-hundred pesos (which was about all I had in my wallet)? For whatever reason, I let Pablo lead me onward.

We walk another three or four blocks and it soon becomes apparent that we are in a part of town where the local junkies and whores hang out. The streets and sidewalks are more busted up than usual. People are standing on corners and leaning up against decrepit buildings. They each possess the tell-tale vacant and restless stare of the drug addict. Toothless old women stand in exaggerated poses, pear-shaped and flabby, swishing tattered skirts this way now that way, hoping to lure the blind or desperate.

It seems Pablo is well-known here. The two women working behind the bar shoot him a look of dread and annoyance. He orders a beer for himself and makes no effort to pay when the woman brings him a bottle.

"You see that girl over there?" He points to a young woman serving drinks to two men who look like they could be cartel members or out-of-work mariachi players. "She'll do you for forty bucks." Her baby blue tights look as if they haven't been washed in weeks. My slight disgust is tempered by the thought that she might very well be living in a ramshackle room with no running water -- and why she's out here, why they're all out here, willing to do the things they do with strange men for a few measly dollars, perhaps a week's wages performing more honest work.

I nod and order myself a beer. The woman returns with a bottle and also charges me for the one that Pablo is drinking.

"You want her, man?" He nudges me with an elbow. "These girls have tight pussies, man! Not like those old hags."

"Nah, I'm good."

He looks at me sideways. "Are you gay?"

"No, man. Just feel like having a drink."

We finish our beers, then he escorts me to another dive across the street.

This place is livelier. There are a number of women sitting at the bar looking bored. Some appear to be missing teeth. Some smile with gold teeth proudly on display. As with the last few places, Pablo orders his drink and heads off to mingle with the place's only attractive girl sitting alone at the far end of the bar. I order a beer for myself and the bartender charges me for both drinks.

What if I said no? What if I told Pablo that I didn't feel like paying for his drinks? What if I had told him to fuck off and stop following me around? Gut instinct tells me our encounter would have ended in an unpleasant fashion -- with Pablo curb-stomping my head outside or beating me senseless with fists like bricks.

This was no paranoid fear. I could see it in Pablo's eyes and in his twitchy mannerisms. This was no half-witted street hustler. I was in the company of a sociopath capable of inflicting much pain and violence. He had mentioned earlier that he once lived in California and how he missed it. I gathered from scattered comments he made while drinking the beers I bought him that life in Cabo hadn't been very kind to Pablo; in fact he looked near homeless in his soiled and stained t-shirt and duct-taped flip-flops. I asked him why he didn't go back.

"I can't go back," he said and went into a convoluted explanation about the status of his citizenship. He spoke perfect English, which indicated to me that he was born and raised in the States. There was a reason he was holed up out here in Cabo. I suspected that reason somehow involved drugs. Or murder.

In the two hours we'd been traipsing about town, Pablo made sure to keep very close to me, within arm's reach. We'd had quite a few beers in that time, and my plan was to wait for it to affect his bladder. I would make my escape as soon as he went to take a leak. But that chance never came.

All that cheap beer was also having an effect on his head. Finally, he left my side and began socializing with the girls at the other end of the bar. He chatted one up in Spanish while draping an arm around the other. Both girls looked annoyed. The prettier one rolled her eyes and shrugged him off. She barked something in Spanish and turned her back to him. Casually, ever so slightly, I took my beer and moved to a bar stool closest to the entrance. I pretended to be fascinated by the porno movies playing on two large flat-screen TVs mounted on the wall directly behind the bar -- two black guys hammering away at some blonde whose breasts were so large and so fake -- violently bouncing around like two over-inflated volleyballs -- that it seemed they would tear right out of her chest with every hip thrust. Two women seated near me -- older hens in their forties or fifties -- giggled and cackled at the gaping, flailing sex organs on the large screen. In-your-face horrific, as American as a monster trucks parked outside a Walmart; McDonald's cheeseburgers and super-sized vanilla milkshakes; morbidly obese women yelling at soiled drooling toddlers, "BLAH BLAH BLAH RAAAWRR!" Squat, shit, repeat.

The entire time I'm watching Pablo out the corner of my eye, still busying himself with the two girls at the other end of the bar. At the moment he seems to have forgotten me, and I take advantage of it. Now's my chance. Slowly....casually....I lean off of my bar stool. And step outside. I look around....just checking the weather....noting the position of the sun. I turn and sprint as fast as I can to the corner, make the turn and keep running, as fast as my flip-flops will take. FLIP-FLAP! FLIP-FLAP! FLIP-FLIP-FLAP! FLIP-FLAP-FLIP!

I turn another corner -- left -- and then another -- right. FLIP-FLAP! FLIP-FLAP-FLIP! FLIP-FLIP-FLAP!

I slow to a walk when I'm a good four or five blocks and a few zig-zagged streets away. Heaving, out of breath -- I glance back. I don't see him. My good friend Pablo. I'm half-expecting to see him coming around the corner, charging after me.

I make it back to our hotel, looking over my shoulder every half-block or so. If there is anything I learned today it is this: it's possible to run at a full sprint in a pair of cheap flip-flops.

Koogmo Thrift & Junk is open for business.

(Crickets chirping.)

Vendors moving out. Empty booths everywhere. The few remaining, like mine, are as voices crying out in the wilderness.

But for $50 a month, it's worth taking a shot to see what sells. Bought a chair from the thrift store down the road for $5. Figure I'll sit out here and rot each weekend. Worst case, I'll get some reading and writing done.

I see a number of electrical outlets. Maybe I'll bring my netbook and play some music while I'm out here.

There are no customers here, only vendors. Not a good sign, but I'll stick it out.

—

Sitting and rotting at the Vikon Flea Market.

Getting a good amount of reading done. Nobody reads anymore. The general public is an increasingly illiterate one. Drooling half-wit mongoloids only interested in buying clothes and music. Or maybe not even that. Who knows what they want? McDonald's cheeseburgers, I guess. And free DVD movies. I'm just waiting to find that one booklover who, like me, goes rummaging through every thrift store on weekends looking for good books.

—

Early Friday evening. This place is a ghost town. The old man across the aisle left for the day. He told me he had a nervous breakdown in 1983. He goes on to say that he struggled for the next seventeen years and tried to kill himself twice. A strange thing to confess to someone at the flea market whom you'd just met the week before.

—

Hung a new sign up at the store today. Black letters on a neon red background. Only open for an hour or so. Got in a little late this afternoon. Probably hang around until 6:30 and then call it a day. As usual, not a single customer. All the other booths are closed.

—

Storm this morning knocked the lights out at the flea market. Vendors standing around in the dark. Ghosts in shadows waiting for the light.

Got the flashlight from the truck and unloaded a few more boxes of books in the dark. Just as I was leaving to get something to eat, the lights came back on.

Got about two full bookshelves full of books now and a few hanging racks of zines and comics. Been sitting here for about two hours now. Not a single customer has come by.

Looks like the old man is recording a commercial to post up on YouTube or wherever. One of the other vendors is recording him with a little camcorder.

The old man said he spoke to Jesus this morning before coming in to the shop. He said, "Jesus, I've been real patient these days. It'd be nice if you could give me a little feedback." He tells me that so far today he's received three inquiries about making custom designs for his t-shirts and hats.

I tell him, "You should sacrifice a goat in the parking lot. I bet you'll get all kinds of business."

He laughs and explains that we are all adopted sons. Whatever that means.

—

Hour two. Or hour three. I've lost count. Time fades into a numb obliviousness. Not a single sale today. Nobody reads anymore. They all watch TV now. Or waste time on the Internet.

There are a lot of people today. Mostly Hispanics and old white people. Do these people read books??

If I didn't' glance at my phone every now and again, I would have no idea what time it was. Vikon Flea Market is as windowless and timeless as a Vegas casino, without the cocktail waitresses and beeping slot machines.

—

Another Friday evening at Koogmo Thrift & Junk. Doesn't seem to be anyone else here. I hear a woman's voice in the next aisle over. I'll hang out for a while longer.

Having this place isn't so much about the retail income as it is a place to sit and rot, zone out, listen to some music and get some writing done.

I hear the rattling of keys and cages closing shut. People closing up shop. This day's a bust.

———

There is an older woman who wanders the aisles. She never really makes eye contact with anyone or smiles; she just sort of stares straight ahead with a distracted, haunted look in her eyes. With long white hair, which she lets hang down past her shoulders, she appears seemingly out of nowhere, quietly drifting by each booth like a ghost. I'm told she's a long-time "close personal friend" of one of the vendors who runs a booth offering electric shock therapy to customers using a device which appears to be made from parts he found at Radio Shack. Every once in a while his lady-friend goes on shoplifting sprees.

Today was one of those days.

She made off with a pair of leather boots from one of the nicer shops, a women's clothing boutique. She didn't just tuck them away and try to sneak off with them, either. She put them on and started walking around the flea market like it was no big deal.

Pauline, the owner of the shop -- everyone calls her "Sexy Pauline" because she dresses real hip and stylish for an older woman -- Pauline goes storming up and down the aisles demanding to see Jamie and Mario, the couple who manage the place. They gathered outside the leasing office, debating what to do about the crazy old woman, who was still walking around with the stolen pair of boots. Evidently, she had lifted a prom dress from another shop the day before (but she wasn't wearing it today).

One of the other vendors came back and said the old woman was spotted headed into the parking lot and off the premises. They all went out to bring her back, not so much to arrest her -- Pauline didn't want to call the cops or put her in jail -- but because it's common knowledge among that the woman's got some kind of mental issues and is borderline homeless (the reason she's always at the flea market is because she's got nowhere else to go).

Pauline got her leather boots back and the old woman returned to her perch in her friend's booth where she assists in handing out business cards and applying that electro-shock therapy to flea market customers.

—

Joe the vinyl record guy came by while I was opening my store. He said he'd brought a ham in for everyone to eat. A ham? Did he slaughter the pig himself? No, those days are over, he says. He bought the ham from the store and decided to bake it for everyone.

"You should swing by and get some," he says. "I put it in Jim's store. You know, the guy who's selling that kid's coffin?"

Jim the antiques guy has been operating a booth at the flea market on and off since 1978. He says he's owned several antiques stores around the Dallas Metroplex. Like many of the other vendors around here, Jim is in his late sixties or early seventies. (I learned later that he was nearly 80.) With deep-set eyes, bushy eyebrows, large teeth, and low rumbling growl of a voice, I get the feeling I'm being addressed by Lurch from the Addams Family.

But Jim's a nice guy. He smiles and welcomes me into his little shop. On the TV in there he's got the Niners-Falcons playoff game on, which is just getting underway. His booth isn't much larger than mine, probably not more than twelve-by-twelve, but it's cozy and has the appearance of someone's living room. On the pegboard walls that have been painted a kind of yellowish-beige hang a few antique looking paintings, the sort you'd see in any Goodwill or Salvation Army store. He's also got a recliner in there, but it's probably not for sale since he's sitting in it in front of the TV. Near the wall I see the child's coffin. It's not a fancy coffin, rather simplistic and unadorned with intricate carvings or details. Just a wooden box that's been stained a dark brown. Somewhat of a morbid item to have as a centerpiece for your store, but there you have it. It's been shoved aside to make room for Joe's ham. Next to that, some paper plates, napkins, and a squeeze bottle of mustard. I dig in and make myself a sandwich. Just like grandma used to make, standing there eating and looking at that child's coffin in Jim's store.

I learn later than Jim's main business isn't selling antiques. He's a practitioner of black magic and self-proclaimed master of the black arts, although you might have been able to surmise as much by the demon skull with horns hanging on the wall in his shop. It's the one thing that kind of sticks out amidst the Goodwill paintings. He says he makes mojo bags and casts spells and removes curses for people. Sometimes I'll stroll past his booth and see him doing readings for clients. He'll have his head down and eyes closed. On the table will be some kind of diagram with a bit of string dangling over it.

—

Five and a half hours -- not a single sale. The little garter snake that Sara found at the park and was planning to keep in the tank in her booth escaped. Went to check on it this morning and it was gone. It must have stood vertical on its tail and slithered through a little opening at the top of the cage.

Coming up on six o'clock. Six hours.

The old Vietnamese lady who runs the shop around the corner asked me what I was doing wasting my time here. "Why aren't you at home helping your wife? You're married, aren't you?"

—

Superbowl Sunday. This place is humming with the silent angst of all the lonely shopkeepers. Next-door Sara brought three of her kids with her today. Her little boy who always smells like shit is crawling around the aisle flinging his little toy skateboard all over the place with a rubberband.

—

The curly-haired husky kid whose mother operates the beads and necklace shop is creeping around like all the other kids whose parents lug them here on the weekends.

He sees me taking a picture of my shop with my new phone.

"What kind of phone is that?" he asks.

"My new iPhone."

"Is it an iPhone 5?"

"iPhone 4."

"Is it a 4s?"

"Nah. I don't like Siri," I tell him. "I don't need to talk to Siri."

"But what about the times for when you feel lonely?"

"That's what girls are for," I wink.

He blushes and runs away.

—

Mazes and bearded weirdos wearing sunglasses. Wasting time and money, and yet we all know that time doesn't exist and money is worthless and nothing ever truly goes to waste because the universe is a closed system, after all. That angst and worry and fretting about and restlessness is all in your fucking head.

—

Going for a stroll through the flea market. Not a customer in sight. The empty aisles prompt quiet reflection. Each little stall reflecting its owners hopes and dreams, their own private realities, bounded by their stall's dimensions -- six by nine, ten by twenty dreams. Quite a few vendors, it seems, have set up their shops more like crazy living spaces than for places of commerce, homes away from home, very little thought given to actually running a profitable business.

I walk by and wave at the old antique dealer sitting in his tiny shop, watching TV with his wife. He smiles and waves back. No words exchanged, just a friendly acknowledgment, and I wonder if this is what a soul experiences when it passes to the other side.

—

90% of the people who come through the flea market are a bunch of Dollar Store derelicts, barely able to keep from pissing and shitting all over themselves, dragging snot-nosed kids and bloated bellies full of McDonald's cheeseburgers and french fries down the narrow, gloomy aisles. They don't know what the hell they're looking at.

—

There's nobody here. Place is a ghost town on Fridays, and it isn't much better on the weekends.

Spent the entire two hours talking to Greg the bookseller -- or rather, being talked at by Greg the bookseller. The guy talks and talks and never shuts up. There is no break in his monologue, no pause, no room for you to slip in a "Well, okay -- I gotta get going." For two hours right up until closing, he wouldn't let me go, and since there wasn't anyone else around, I was stuck. He talked about his books (an impressive collection, to be honest). He talked about the sewer line he had to repair at his house. He talked about the years he spent working at a flea market in Arkansas (he sold bill folds and men's wallets). Then back to books. Then his collection of Beanie Babies. Not a pause or moment to catch his breath in any of this. He talked and talked and talked. This was no conversation because there was no talking back. It was just one long continuous stream-of-consciousness rambling recounting of his own life and times. No feedback required. No response necessary.

There was no way to bow out gracefully. No way to politely excuse myself. Finally, I just said: "I gotta get going. See you later." and half-ran, half-walked back to my shop. I left him still recounting the plot of some late-night horror movie he'd been watching the week before. I could hear him talking as I was walking away. It was as if I didn't even need to be there. He might as well have been talking to himself. Maybe this entire time, he was.

—

First encounter with someone suffering from multiple personality disorder at the flea market today. Or demonic possession.

Dan's been having problems paying his booth fees and making sales. Business partner bailed out on him last week.

So I'm standing there talking to him. Says he doesn't see a way out of it. $8k in debt. I say, So move into a smaller booth. Dan's mumbling something about how Jesus has abandoned him and how he's been thinking about killing himself again. I say, Don't do that. Then all of a sudden, his head slumps down against his chest. I'm thinking he's fainted or something. He's an old guy, in his 70's. He comes to and stares me square in the eyes. "Dan's not here anymore," he says. He looks and sounds different now. Fucking goosebumps.

I say, Where's Dan? "Dan's hiding in the corner. I've been in control for 33 years."

Granted, I've only known Dan for about three months, but he LOOKED and SOUNDED different. His eyes had grown dark. Not being a religious person, I mumbled something like, To deny Jesus is to deny life. You kill yourself, you pay the ultimate penalty. Dan, or whatever was in control of Dan, shouted back: "THE LORD HAS ABANDONED US AND I AM IN CONTROL NOW."

I fuckin' got the hell outta there. Unfortunately, my booth is right next to his. I sat there for an hour or so, listening as "Dan" rambled on to anyone about being abandoned by God and "his bastard son." "Dan" is no longer the feeble and meek Dan that I'm familiar with. This guy is standing with his chest out and gesturing dramatically. This Dan is going on and on about how God has abandoned "them" and how Jesus owes "them" for 33 years of misery.

I go over to Joe's booth. "You gotta go see Dan. He's talking to himself in the third person and sounds and looks different." Joe says, "Nuh-uh. I ain't going over there. I had a sister who went nuts. I know what that's like."

Dan is beginning to attract attention from the other vendors, yelling about God and everything. This isn't how he usually is. I tell Sara, who runs the booth across from mine: "You got any holy water? Maybe we should spray him." Turns out, Sara does have some holy water. In fact, she's got a jar full of the stuff. "Don't laugh at me! I'm a Catholic!" she says. So Sara goes into Dan's store and starts sprinkling her jar of holy water all over his stuff. He's too busy rambling about Jesus to notice.

The rest of us gather around to decide what to do. The African lady points a finger at me: "He went crazy when you told him he shouldn't be selling his hats or t-shirts. I heard you!" Not true, I say. I only told him he should condense his stuff and move into a smaller space. Dan's store looks like crap. There's garbage all over the place. Looks like a hoarder lives there. Or a pack rat.

Somehow they elect me as the one who needs to go into the leasing office and ask them to call the cops. "He's gonna kill himself. We can't let that happen." "We can't let him drive. He might run over a family." I'm of the sole opinion that we can't force him to do anything and we should just let him go. But no, we have to call the cops.

"Nobody normal would ever come here," says Joe, as I'm pouring my glass of vodka.

Just another nut at the flea market.

—

Dan had another mental episode at the flea market today. I came in at around noon and one of the old guys who runs the tool shop was standing out in the aisle. "Watch out," he said grinning as I passed. "Don't go near your store." I turn the corner and there's Dan, hollering and swearing at the top of his lungs. Evidently, he got into again with another old guy he's been having issues with for the past few weeks.

First some background. This other guy -- an old ponytailed fellow who regularly comes into the flea market limping around on a handcrafted, twisted and gnarled wooden cane -- this guy, according to Dan, wanted to sell Dan a handgun for two hundred dollars. Dan says he was interested in the handgun but wasn't ready to buy anything just yet. The ponytailed fellow went ahead and brought the gun in one day and demanded payment for it, to which Dan said he had changed his mind and didn't want to buy it anymore. This angered the ponytailed old man and since that day he'd been leaving nasty handwritten notes taped to the front of Dan's store, notes stating something to the effect: "THE OWNER OF THIS STORE IS A LIAR AND A CHEAT!" or "RIPOFF! DON'T BUY ANYTHING FROM THIS MAN!"

Today Dan apparently confronted the man about the nasty notes he'd been leaving on Dan's store, and that's when Dan's other, more assertive personality, George, took over. It was George that was doing all the yelling and cursing.

I was opening my shop, and Dan/George came stomping down the aisle. "Hey, Dan," I said, "You all right?"

"I don't have time for you right now, Anthony," said Dan/George. "I'll return control to Dan when I'm done handling this situation."

"OK," I said. "I'll be here if you need anything."

"I appreciate it," said Dan/George. Then he handed me a piece of candy.

The police were called (again), and they interviewed Dan and the ponytailed gentleman. Although the ponytailed old man has a concealed carry license, guns are not allowed on the premises, something that the police informed him of today. Also, he is not to go anywhere near Dan's store, although he will be allowed to frequent other shops at the flea market.

I'm wondering now if I need to wear a bullet-proof vest to sell my books and typewriters.

—

A guy was sitting in Dan's store today, talking about Israel and gun control. We seem to get a lot of those types coming through the flea market -- guys who are always willing to talk guns and Mid-East politics. Usually white, probably conservative, and usually in their fifties or sixties.

The guy says to Dan, "Guns aren't the problem. It's all the crazy people. Crazy people are the problem."

The guy doesn't realize he's talking to a diagnosed schizophrenic with multiple personalities.

—

Sold a chess set and a Blondie album today. It's a damn good day when I sell anything at all. Two more people asked about my typewriters. Those old typers attract more interest than anything else in my store.

—

The woman who sells clothes came by my store today. "Your store is always so cozy and romantic," she says, "Wait, I tell you that all the time, don't I?"

I blush and say thanks. (She never buys anything.)

—

My friend Joe from Round 'N Round Records closed up his booth, but he asked if I wanted to take some of his albums on consignment. Sell them for $5 to $10 in my store. I said, You think these flea market cheapskates are gonna pay $5 to $10 for an album? I was asking $4 for that Blondie record, but some kid offered $2. I said, What the hell and sold it for $2. Who cares?

We operate on small margins out here in the scavenger badlands of Vikon Village. Very small margins.

I'm in my shop the other day talking about UFOs and reincarnation with one of my customers. He's telling me how aliens are kidnapping humans and–

First, let me back up....

It seems the latest issue of my newsletter, Koogmo #5, has created some controversy at the flea market. I'm summoned to the leasing office first thing Saturday. Inside, Mario is sitting on the couch, along with his pregnant teenage daughter who is sitting behind the desk. We are joined shortly by Mario's wife, Lucinda.

I glance around, "Uh-oh. Am I in trouble?"

Their daughter, in an authoritative tone, hands me a copy of Koogmo #5. "You want to explain this?" I see sections of it highlighted in yellow.

"What do you mean?" I say.

She wanted to know why I was writing about people in the flea market and why I was portraying Vikon Village in a negative light. She tells me I can't do that.

"Those are just stories I'm telling."

"Well, you can't be writing about other people without their permission."

"I changed the names."

"But we know who you're talking about, and why didn't you change the name of Vikon Flea Market?"

I say to her: "When's the last time you read a book?"

"I don't have time to read," she says. And I believe it, as disappointed as I am whenever I hear that sort of statement. She is quite obviously pregnant. With her protruding belly, I always see her pushing a stroller through the flea market with her two other children, an infant and a toddler. She can't be more than eighteen or nineteen. Still a baby herself.

"Or a magazine? Or a newspaper?"

"I don't have time to read," she says.

"Have you ever heard of the First Amendment?"

She shakes her head.

"Or the Freedom of Speech?"

She shakes her head. "Look, you can't be doing this. Why did you use the flea market's real name? Why did you change everyone else's name except the flea market? Don't you realize that makes us look bad?"

"These are just stories I write. I'm going to write whatever I feel I need to write."

"Well, you've been writing about people, and they don't like it."

"Who?"

"I'm not going to tell you who. But let me just say this: We can't guarantee your safety if you continue writing about the people here."

"Guarantee my safety?" I'm sitting there looking at a very pregnant teenaged mother with two kids who doesn't have time to read. "Thanks, but I don't think I need your protection."

Her mother chimes in. "Why do you write about the crazy man and the man with the gun?"

"It was an interesting story, one that I thought was worth telling. Also, I was there when it happened."

"What if the man with the gun comes back to shoot you?"

I shrug. "There's not much I can do about that, is there?"

"But you can't talk about the crazy man. It's not your business."

"Sure I can. These things happened in public, in a public setting, right in front of me. It's not like I was peeking into the man's house or breaking into the hospital and publishing his medical records."

The mother and daughter are exasperated. They're firing words back and forth in Spanish. Meanwhile, Mario is sitting on the couch. He's looking at me and smiling as wide as a sombrero. Finally, the mother says they're done with me and says we'll talk again next week. She waves me out the door.

I'm beginning to think they're going to ask me to close up my shop and leave the flea market. I'm also beginning to think maybe they're right. I probably shouldn't be writing about people in the flea market and then leaving copies in my store for everyone to read. In future issues, I resolve to change Vikon Flea Market to Viking Flea Market. I had intended to call it something else, but I just plain forgot. And quite honestly, I didn't think anyone would give a shit.

I'm trying to remember what I wrote. I mean, I remember the overall gist of each issue, but I don't always recall the exact words or stories. By the time I've written the stuff, printed it out and published it, it's gone from my mind. Purged. Like a snake crawling out of its own dead skin. I've already moved onto my next writing project.

Later back at my store, I'm sitting there with Joe, the old guy who used to buy records but never had anything for sale. He only buys. He'd leave little Post-It Notes all over his store informing customers that nothing was for sale -- he only BUYS records. He says he's got a second house filled with about a million albums he's collected over the years. He still comes around to hang out. In fact, I've taken up the spot where his old place used to be. In his opinion, Koogmo #5 is a classic.

"I'm going to have to go back and re-read it," I tell him. "I don't remember saying anything that was too insulting."

"You said Suzy's kid always smells like shit. You said Greg talks too much and never shuts up. You said the place is a ghost town and customers are idiots," says Jack, "The one about the kid smelling like shit, that one cracked me up. I was sitting in bed at 11 o'clock at night reading it and I just started busting out laughing."

"I didn't mean to hurt anyone's feelings."

"Oh, of course."

"I was just writing whatever came to mind and trying to be as honest as possible about it."

"You're like that final episode of 'Seinfeld.' You can't understand why everyone hates you. Did you see that episode?"

"Yeah."

"It was hilarious."

But Koogmo #5 is not without its supporters. A few vendors came up to me and said they liked my style of writing. The old antiques dealer and practitioner of the black arts says to me, "I like your way with words, baby boy." He asked me to write his biography, wants me to tell his story about the days he spent working on a stud farm in the 50s and 60s, where he and a handful of other men serviced lonely Dallas socialites.

The woman next door said she and her daughter were cracking up in their shop reading what I'd written. They partnered up with another older woman who overhears what we're talking about. She picks up a copy of Koogmo #5 out of curiosity.

She's flipping through the pages and as she's reading along, she pops her head into my shop: "Oh, this stuff is funny!"

Five minutes later: "This should be a movie. Do you know anyone in show business?"

Two minutes after that: "You know, if you ever hope to get this published you need to tone down all the cussing and swearing."

She comes around again: "You know, this should be published in book form, so it looks more professional." She's standing there, dangling my newsletter by the stapled corner.

"That's by design," I tell her. "I try to keep things as simple as possible. It's made to be rolled up and stuffed in back pockets or stashed in backpacks. It can even be used as emergency toilet paper!"

"And if you can make the font just a little bit bigger. It's too hard to read."

It is all just so much crap, anyway. Nothing more annoying than a wannabe writer more concerned about the format of his precious words than the actual words themselves. Look at all the self-published "books" that are out there now. By the usually shitty cover alone, you can judge a self-published book a mile away -- they have that generically vanilla look to them. You know when their owners have given up on making the bestseller list because you'll see stacks of his self-published tripe piled high in the book sections of Goodwill stores and other thrift shops. I doubt the stuff will sell even there. It would have been more efficient and time-consuming if they had just tossed them straight into the dumpsters out back.

The woman comes by a few minutes later, smiling wryly. "You know, I have also been known to dabble in the written word."

Aww, shit....here it comes.

"I write poetry," she says.

Fuck. I knew it. Another gifted soul, touched by an angel.

She takes out her cell phone and shows me a photo of what appears to be a Thomas Kinkade painting. "I wrote a poem about this and it took second place in a contest. Maybe I'll bring some of my poems by."

"Sure," I say. "We'll have a poetry reading right here in my store. We'll serve alcohol and play jazz records."

What does it matter? The leasing office will probably be kicking me out since I've been accused of writing disparaging comments about the flea market and its people.

I debated whether to open the shop the next day, or ever again.

"Why even go there if people hate you now?" says the wife. "You're not even making any money. You're just wasting your time."

But I decide against such rational logic and open my store promptly at noon the next day. Business is business and if that place has turned into my own personal ass-kicking machine, then so be it. Might as well take my lumps now and get it over with.

I spend most of the day waiting to be attacked and instead end up talking to an old white-haired Hispanic guy whose low guttural growl I first mistook as a Russian accent. He bought the toilet trophy my wife won at a benefit tournament at a pool hall a few years back. Beneath the small bronze toilet, a little plaque reads "PLAYED LIKE S**T." Sold it to him for three bucks.

"What goes into the bowl?" he asks, inspecting the trophy from various angles.

"I dunno. My wife used it for an ashtray."

"I'll put a little doll in there or something."

The woman next door pops her head into my shop. She's holding a large binder against her chest. I wave and smile at her. Seeing me with a customer, she smiles and ducks back into her store.

The old man asks about the Buddhist chant CDs I have stacked near the music CDs. He wants to give them a listen before buying one, but I don't have a CD player.

"I only like the woman voice," he says, "I don't like the man voice."

"I don't know. But they're a dollar each. Are you Buddhist?"

"No, but I like to listen to women chanting in the background."

So we start talking about religion and reincarnation and God. He believes everything, and so do I. As we're talking, he's looking through all my occult books -- *Crystal Power, Pyramid Healing*, etc.

From the corner of my eye I see the woman next door peeking into my shop. She's still clutching that binder to her chest.

Then the old man starts telling me about UFOs, and I tell him about my experiences. His eyes widen, "You've seen those things?"

"Yes!"

"Oh, man. You are so lucky."

He tells me that aliens are living amongst us and some even occupy high levels of government.

"I believe it!" I say.

He leans toward me. "And do you know, they've been kidnapping people. Not just thousands. Not just tens of thousands. That's what the reports tell us, but the reality is....these aliens have kidnapped up to a million people."

"Holy shit."

I see the woman with her binder again, hovering near the entrance of my shop.

"You know what they're doing? They're kidnapping us and grinding us into powder so they can eat us."

"But why?"

He shrugs. "They need nutrients or something."

"That makes sense," I tell him. "After all, we are made of the same components that make the stars and planets in this universe -- carbon, nitrogen, hydrogen, whatever. So instead of collecting it from around the universe, they just collect it from us."

"Yes! And did you know--"

The woman barges into the shop. She can't wait any longer. "Excuse me, just real quick," she says, holding a finger up to the man. She turns to me, "I just wanted to read you this poem."

The man looks at her then looks at me, puzzled.

"It's about books." She begins reading from her binder: "Books should be cherished. Books bring us joy, laughter, and even adventure. Books can be held and loved. Indeed, they are as our children. Each one..."

And on and on....

When she's finished, I tell her that we were just discussing UFOs and reincarnation.

"Oh, none of that stuff is true!" She turns to the man and says, "Do you accept Jesus Christ as your Lord and Savior?"

"Listen, lady," he says, "do you believe we human beings are the only ones in the universe?"

The woman holds up her finger. "Do you accept the Bible as the word of God?"

The old man waves her off. "Oh, please! The Bible was written by men!"

I leave them to their discussion and head down to the Mexican cafe to order some tacos. I glance at my phone. It's already 3 o'clock. I've been talking to this guy for nearly three hours. When I return with my food a few minutes later, my shop is empty and quiet. I take my seat behind the glass counter and eat my tacos.

And I wait. I wait to be attacked by angry flea market vendors, women with binders full of poetry, or aliens from other dimensions.

They're trying to turn us into insects. Like busy little worker bees. Ants always on the move. Everyone crawling up each other's asses every goddamn day. It's fucking retarded. The college grads and new hires seem to like it. Maybe it's because they don't know any better or maybe it's because they're reluctant to say otherwise.

Management gutted the test teams last October. They fired my manager, his boss, and my manager's boss's boss. They also let go of a handful of grunts who were underperforming or whose work was "no longer beneficial to the company." They hit us across the board in four different states.

We all saw it coming. Company was planning to move the entire business unit to the Agile method of software development. A meaningless concept for people who don't work in the industry, but what it is essentially, is instead of giving individuals a chunk of work to do and then sending them off to their respective cubicles to go work for the next few months, reporting back every so often (what is frowned upon as the 'waterfall' method), the Agile process requires people to work in teams of four or five, who must meet face-to-face every day and scribble what they're doing on Post-It Notes, which are then posted up on whiteboards in various conference rooms for management to see. It's meant to be highly collaborative and iterative, where people are expected to "swarm" around tasks to get them completed.

I have grown too accustomed to working alone in near isolation.

More cynical employees see it as puerile micro-managing. The new ones appear more hopeful. One of my coworkers, a new hire right out of college, commented the other day: "I've been here seven months! It goes by so quickly."

I'm sitting there thinking: "I should have quit two years ago."

I was burned out the day I started. I've been meaning to quit work, period, since 1996 when my days working late nights as a litigation paralegal came to an end. I have grown weary of having to learn new things just for the sake of learning something new. I have grown weary of having to devote time and energy to trivial tasks which contain very little meaning other than a need to earn a paycheck to put food on the table. I have grown weary of sitting in front of a computer monitor or laptop screen, typing endlessly on little plastic keyboards. Carpal tunnel syndrome has plagued me since my first real typing job working as a docket clerk twenty years ago. Back when I thought computers were fun. Back when I used to write little screensavers in QBasic on my 386 PC with 4MB of RAM and an 80MB hard drive. That's what software development basically boils down to: endless typing on little plastic keyboards.

Feeling tired. I want to get away and spend my time daydreaming or sitting in quiet contemplation. I want to relax and take my time. I want to practice kindness toward small animals. I want to indulge my curiosities at a leisurely pace. Slowly evolving and growing. Better to slow everything down to the point of absolute stillness, like a zen monk in quiet meditation, contemplating The Void. Be deliberate and meaningful. All in due time. Never, NO more, that rush Rush RUSH! Must get HERE! Or THERE! Quickly! Quickly! Deadlines! Schedules! STAY COMPETITIVE!

Yeah. No, thanks. I no longer enjoy my job. But I still have to work, right? Of course. A childish question, but sometimes it is the childish questions that prompt the soul-searching and cause us to see modern living for the farce and falsity it has become.

Ask stupid questions. If all you receive are stupid answers then the entire thing needs to be thrown out. Start over. Recast the stones across the dusty ground and see what comes up.

This week I had hoped to be a good employee -- what our business unit calls "contributors." I was planning to contribute. I got to my cube Monday morning but for some reason didn't feel like going to our daily meeting at 10:45. I didn't feel like going to any meetings. Instead, I left for lunch. I forgot what I had. I may have just gone home and took a nap. Came back to the office at about 1:30, checked my inbox and found a meeting invite to "Discuss new user story" scheduled for 2 o'clock. I didn't feel like discussing anything, so I left and drove to the thrift store. I went home from there, took another nap, then took the dogs for a walk later that evening.

I was a little slow in getting up Tuesday morning. It's the middle of summer, and the days are warm and sunny. Meditative. Driving into the office, my daughter calls and asks me to pick her up from her friend's house. She had spent the night. I glance at my phone. 9:30. My phone starts buzzing again. I recognize the number. My manager is calling me. I let it go to voicemail. I check it a few moments later. He's asking if I was on vacation yesterday and if I plan to be on vacation today. I play the message for my daughter, and we both laugh.

I didn't call my manager back. I went into the office. A few of my coworkers are standing around in a group outside one of the cubes. They spot me and I wave to them. I login to my laptop and see a chat message from my manager timestamped around 4 o'clock yesterday afternoon. I close the chat window and submit a vacation request for yesterday and -- well, hell....might as well take another vacation today, too. I leave for home and then spend the rest of the day hanging out in Dallas. Went to another one of my thrift stores on Harry Hines, thinking to myself: "Soon I will not be able to pay for any of this. I won't have a job, and I'll be broke." I bought a $4 pair of flip-flops.

My wife sees me when she gets home from her job, "You didn't go to work again? Oh my God. You're gonna get fired."

"I know," I say. "I'm probably going to quit this week."

We both laugh.

With the Agile process, Wednesdays are the big meeting days. We all sit in a large conference room. There are about thirty of us in there, split into four teams. Each team must give a brief demonstration of the work they've been doing from the previous two weeks. Then we talk about what we learned, what could be improved, what didn't work so well. All of it utterly pointless bullshit. Then we reconvene after lunch and pick new tasks to work on for the next two weeks. It's like fuckin' fifth grade all over again. I spend most of my time sitting in those meetings bored out of my mind. We don't even have a window to stare out of.

I made a genuine effort to go into the office on Wednesday, but as I was backing the truck out of the garage I discovered that my left rear tire had gone flat. I put on the spare then drove to Firestone to have the flat repaired. Must be something about Texas and my truck, but I get two or three flat tires every year. Or perhaps it is the Universe calling out to me: Forget your job. Go find something else to do.

Firestone would repair the tire for free, and in the meantime I sent an email to my manager informing him that I got a flat tire and would be in a little late.

Waiting for my tire, I strolled around the little strip mall. It was still too early. Most of the shops were closed. Across the parking lot outside the Aldi's grocery store, I spotted a red bird laying on the pavement, just a few feet from the automatic sliding door entrance. It was quivering and appeared to be in pain. I thought to take a picture of it with my iPhone but decided it would be disrespectful given the state of suffering it was in. It seemed to be readying itself for death. I bundled it up in my handkerchief and carried it around the corner. There was still some life in it as it struggled to get free a few times. I set it beneath a patch of bushes along K Avenue, leaving my handkerchief with it.

My tire was fixed by 9:30, but instead of rushing to work, I went home and made lunch plans with my daughter. We ate ramen at a Japanese noodle joint down the street from our house. Then I dropped her off at her friend's house and drove back to Dallas. Never did make it into the office that day.

That afternoon, I received two calls from work. I let both go to voicemail. I was afraid to listen to them until I got home later that evening at which time I played them back in front of my wife. One was from my manager asking if I planned to be on vacation the rest of the week. The other was from my manager's manager, the "engineering development prime" of the project we're working on. He wanted to know if everything was okay and that I could feel free to call him on his cell phone to discuss anything if I wanted.

These are nice people. I felt bad. I got all teary-eyed when I listened to that message from my manager's manager. I had worked with him for close to six years before our business unit migrated to the Agile process. The reality was that they were probably already preparing my severance package, and if I were to quit it would make it that much easier on them.

But I had already made up my mind: It is time to take my leave of Cisco Systems. This nine-year ride has come to an end for me. I can no longer do the work. I can no longer keep up with the pace. Actually, I can – I just don't care. Life is short, and my concerns and curiosities have taken me elsewhere, far away from the cubicles of Corporate America. I'm forty-four years old, and there is a big beautiful world out there that I've been meaning to see. You can't see it sitting in a cube or stuck in windowless conference rooms all day. No, I needed to get the hell out of there.

Thursday morning I awoke smiling with excited anticipation. The beginning, the frightening beginning, was this close. One more step to carry this thing through to The End. Today was the day I would submit my resignation. I've been a working stiff for twenty some-odd years. I've quit my share of jobs. Been fired once, even. But I've not quit a job I've had for this long (9 years) and with such financial consequences at stake. But a job is still just a job, and life is eternal. This I held in my mind like a candle flame in meditation.

Drinking my coffee in front of my computer at home, I see a Reuters article saying "Cisco Systems is planning to layoff 6,000 employees." I disregard it. I thought about waiting around for a layoff package but decided the undetermined time to wait isn't worth the mental anguish of having to work with a bunch of people I don't particularly care to work with on a daily basis. Better to jump now while I have the gumption and momentum. Anyway, the article mentions cloud computing is what Cisco will be spending their money on, something I already know since it's the group I'm working in. I should be excited to be a part of this cutting edge technology, but no, I would rather go to truck driving school and learn how to drive an 18-wheeler across the country. Or maybe buy a trailer in a trailer park somewhere and go work as a dishwasher where people will assume I don't speak English and leave me alone. Save up whatever money I can scrape together and go traveling whenever I felt like it. Something like that. Need to find the sort of gig where I'm left alone. No one bothering me every fucking day. No managers, no product owners, no architects or scrum team members trying to crawl up my ass.

Okay, maybe it's not that bad, but it has certainly come to feel that way more often than not.

As soon as I got to the office, I went to my cube and quickly bundled up my laptop, cables, power supply, and docking station and moved down to the second-floor lab space where nobody sits anymore. Just a few years ago this place was humming with racks of servers, routers, switches, and all the people working on them. Now it's just a large, darkened area with rows and rows of empty lab benches. There in the dark with just a bit of morning light coming through the windows, I set up my laptop. Why, I'm not sure. I think I was afraid to see any of my coworkers from the fourth floor. At least not until I submitted my resignation to my manager, who also sits on the fourth floor.

I logged in, saw that he was online and sent him an instant message asking if he had a quick minute to chat. Sure, stop by, he replies.

Bracing myself now. Butterflies in my gut. I'm about to walk away from a six-figure salary with little more than a year's worth of savings in the bank. Fuck it.

I'm waiting at the elevators when Tina, one of the project managers, comes around the corner buried beneath her usual pile of stuff -- department store shopping bag, backpack, purse, sweater, coat thrown over her shoulder. She's like a walking luggage cart. She always looks like she's running away.

"Hey," she says, "where you been?"

"Oh, you know....just hanging out."

She leans in close and whispers, "You didn't hear it from me, but people been talking. They say you're never around anymore."

"I decided to take a few days off."

"Be careful. Management is watching."

"Yeah, I know. I'm on my way out. Gonna submit my resignation today."

Her eyes widen. "Don't do that, dude! Didn't you hear about the layoffs? Wait for The Package!"

A severance package is what people in the company refer to as "The Package." It typically includes three months of severance pay, plus additional pay for however many years you've been with the company, plus a one-year extension of your health benefits. Or something like that.

She hops into the elevator and rides with me to the fourth floor. "It's free money, dude. Just wait. Try to hang in there!"

I tell her I'll think about it, but I've pretty much made up my mind. At this point, I'm willing to walk away from all of it. It's been a long, difficult year. A lot of shit went down, and I need some time to decompress. And I mean TIME. Six months. A year. Who knows how long. Need to get away for a bit. Do some wandering and thinking.

I get to my manager's office, and he's staring at the screen on his laptop.

"John's video conference is about to start," he says. "Are you going to watch?"

"What's it about?"

"You didn't hear? He's going to talk about the restructuring. They sent out the invite yesterday -- oh, but you weren't here."

"Right."

The "John" he's referring to is the CEO of the company. You can tell if you're talking to someone in management or just a lowly grunt by the way they refer to people losing their jobs. Managers will always call it a "restructuring."

"What'd you want to talk about?" He's typing and logging into the online video conference. "Is it something critical?"

"No, not really," I say. "We can talk later."

"Okay, good. Let's meet later this afternoon."

So I head down to the second floor lab, gather my things, and bring them back to my cube up on the fourth floor. One of my coworkers pokes her head into my cube, "Hey, you're back."

I take my usual three-hour lunch. At around two o'clock, I get back to the office.

My manager leans back in his chair and crosses his legs. "So. What's up? We've been wondering where you've been."

"Decided to take a few days off. You know, since it was innovation week last week and the end of the sprint."

"Oh, I see. So it was the end of the sprint and there wasn't much work for you to do?"

"Right."

"In the future, if you could please let your teammates know where you are."

"Sure."

"Or, if you can just call me on my cell phone. That way, I can relay the message for you."

"Will do."

"Because your behavior seems very strange. Everybody is wondering where you are, what you're doing."

I feel like I'm talking to the villain in a kung-fu movie. I laugh. Then he starts laughing. I think we both realize the futility of this conversation.

"So what was it you wanted to see me about?"

The cliches spill from my mouth like damp cardboard: "I heard someone on the automation team left last week. I believe I would be a much stronger contributor if I transitioned to that team. I would have a beneficial impact on productivity."

"Hmm, that seems like a good idea. Let me ask around and see if we can work something out."

So it's back to business as usual. I rejoin my team in our daily scrum meetings, take on a few tasks and user stories, making sure to write whatever it is the hell I'm doing on Post-It Notes and posting them up to the whiteboard. At the Wednesday meeting, some of the guys from the other scrums greet me: "Hey, you're still here?" "Long time no see." "You're alive!"

I feel like someone who has died and is now viewing his former existence from another dimension with bemused detachment. At least I still have a paycheck coming in.

———

P.S., It's been a week and still no signs of layoffs. It's like waiting for a mafia hit. Until then, I still have a job and I still take three-hour lunch breaks. Rumors are swirling. People in hallways are whispering. Soon.

———

P.S.S., Fast forward one month...I can't believe I got an end-of-year bonus. I was thinking for sure I wouldn't get one this time around. It would have been the first time in my nine years at Cisco that I didn't get one, but I did. Go figure. I laughed when my manager handed me my bonus letter.

"You sure this isn't a mistake?" I ask.

"It's not all bad news," he says straight-faced, still sounding like a kung-fu villain.

—

Two weeks later: My manager sets up a last minute one-on-one meeting first thing in the morning. We usually have a one-on-one every month, and we'd just had a meeting the week before. I know what this one is about. This is it. Here it comes. What I've been waiting for, what I've been planning for and expecting.

He waits for me to shut the door. Then proceeds: "First I need to read this to you."

"Ahh...I know what this is about."

"You do? Okay, well let me read this first. 'As you know, Cisco is implementing a restructuring...blah blah blah....I regret to inform you....blah blah blah....please note that this was a business decision and not a personal one...blah blah blah...'"

Tina was right. Good thing I waited. Free money. It was the usual payout -- three months severance plus a six-week lump sum payout to cover health benefits.

All I need now is a plane ticket. But first I need to return the company laptop.

The old lady who sometimes hangs out with the two old guys that sell tools stopped me on my way into my shop this morning. She's always sporting such a bright happy smile for someone missing most of her front teeth.

"You wanna buy a shirt?" she says, smiling and leaning into me. "How big is your neck? 16?"

"I don't know," I say.

"17? You're about the same size as my ex-husband. You're probably a 17. You've never measured your own neck?"

"No."

"Well, you look like you got a big neck, like my ex-husband. You're probably a 17. You sure you don't want a shirt? Only a dollar!"

"No thanks." Then I start laughing and smiling. That smile of hers is so infectious.

—

Joe stopped by my shop yesterday. I told him I haven't made my booth fee since moving into the spot he vacated last May. No surprise, of course. It's as we had discussed previously -- people don't operate the booths at this flea market to make money. No, there must be some other reason. Something psychological, perhaps. Or maybe something which stems from feelings of loneliness and some subconscious need to connect with other people. Whatever the reason, here we are -- me, Joe, and all the rest of the lonely flea market lunatics -- sitting in our little metal cage shops, prison cells without the locks, each of us tending to our own private world of hopes and dreams made public Friday through Sunday each week in the form of knick-knacks, trinkets, and dolls; used books and dresses; second-hand pornography and Goodwill paintings; Hot Wheels and antique Asian collectibles.

All the stuff is there to give us a reason to be there. The ones who open up shop solely to make money rarely stay very long because there is no money to be made. Many of them realize this by the second or third month. They'll come in on a Friday at the end of the month and sheepishly pack their stuff out. Those of us who remain are like ghosts, lonely souls with nothing better to do, nowhere to go. The place is a backwater tidepool. Week after week you see the same fish and sea urchins. Wave "hi" to the hermit crabs and nod "hello" to grumpy seagulls. Let's see what the tide brings in today.

I'll have been running my shop a year this coming January, and in that time I've developed my own set of regulars and semi-regulars, hardly a one ever buying anything. Most come by simply to hang out and chat, which is fine with me. Times like these I feel I become more therapist than flea market vendor. I sit behind my glass counter and listen to them tell me their life stories, sometimes for hours. Sitting quietly, I allow myself to become a sounding board for their thoughts and impressions. I've discovered that the more long-winded ones rarely ask how I'm doing or how my life is going, which may not indicate callousness or self-centeredness on their part; it may be due simply to the perception that the therapist never needs therapy. They see my store is open. They see me standing there. They figure everything must be okay.

As I imagine it is with patients so it is with my customers -- each has their own recurring theme or issue they are trying to work through week after week.

—

Edgar is in his eighties and tells me about his adventures with the women the government sends to cook and clean for him. When his wife of many years died in 2006, the government started sending a home-care aide to his house for a few hours each day.

I met him within the first month of opening my shop. I noticed him browsing through the comic books I had for sale along the wall. He was thumbing through some of the dirtier, "adult-only" issues, the ones with large-breasted, half-naked women on the covers. "You got any more like these?" he says. "I like these kinds of comic books with strong women."

He bought two dollars worth of comics that day.

Over the course of the next year, he'd stop by my shop every Saturday. Every once in a while he'd ask if I had gotten any more comics in. One day I showed him a box of old VHS porn tapes I bought from another vendor. He dug through the pile, carefully inspecting each one, taking his time to read the blurb on the back of each box. "I only like the ones with stories," he said. "You know fantasy type stories, with strong women. I like strong women."

He bought two dollars worth of porn that day.

He's a sharp-witted, sharp-tongued guy, highly intelligent and filled with more energy and life than many people half his age. He taught aircraft and automotive repair in his younger days and is himself a licensed pilot. He explains auto mechanics and aircraft technology with a fiery temperament. One week he would be lecturing me on the inner workings of a manual transmission versus an automatic. The next week, he'd be telling me about the difficulties of trying to land a small plane on the side of a mountain on a windy day. Whenever I asked him a stupid question, which was often, he would narrow his eyes at me and say, "Son, is your head on right? Because I don't think it is. You need to start paying attention."

He has two sons. "My two boys," as he refers to them. One "boy" is a pilot for United Airlines and is nearing sixty years old. His other "boy," a few years younger than the pilot, lives in Wills Point and spends his time traveling to flea markets and fairs setting up and repairing large canvas tents. He says I remind him of his younger son: "You want to do a lot of things...this and that...but you don't have the damndest idea how to go about doing any of it...you just kinda make things up as you go, don't ya?"

And he loves his black women. All except one of his home-care aides was a black woman, he tells me, and he'll have it no other way. He tells me their stories. They all seem to have five or six boyfriends, he says, and just as many kids. They all know how to work the welfare system -- how to give the right answers, how to turn food stamps into cash, who to call, when to call, and where to go to get what you need. "It's a complicated process," he tells me, "but it works. These women know how to make it work." He leans back and folds his arms, chuckling on the other side of the glass counter. "I find it fascinating," he says.

The weekend following Thanksgiving, I asked him how his holiday went. It seemed an innocent question, but maybe I should have been more sensitive. He furrowed his brows. "I fired my worker," he says.

"The one you hired just last week?"

"Yep. Got rid of her."

"What happened?"

"You know it was Thanksgiving, right?"

"Yeah."

"The gal came by in the morning. She left me two sandwiches on the counter. Couple pieces of white bread with cheese and a few slices of ham. She was in a rush to get out of there." He looks down and shakes his head. "On Thanksgiving Day."

Another time, he told me about a woman he fired because she didn't want to be seen with him in public. Perhaps he is a bit disheveled looking, lurching with bushy gray eyebrows and liver spots, but not particularly unattractive, just a typical grumpy old man. Most times I saw him at my shop at the flea market, he was wearing the same gray t-shirt that read "Parkland Hospital."

"I tell these gals that work for me," he says. "If you're gonna be shopping with me at the store, I want you to walk next to me. Not fifty feet behind me. And none of that 'Meet me outside when you're done' stuff. You need to be next to me."

I realized then that the women sent to his house meant a little more to him than just hired help sent to do his cooking and cleaning.

"Maybe that's the problem," I say.

"What is?"

"These women are professionals, and they're trying to maintain a professional relationship. Maybe they feel a little uncomfortable when you try to make it more personal."

"Good point," he says, stroking the random gray hairs on his chin. "I did not consider that."

Then he shows me photos he took of some of the women with his old flip phone. They're posing provocatively on his back porch. "Here, this one's my favorite," he says. He shows me a low-resolution photo of a large black woman hiking her skirt up and arching her back with her butt out. "Oh, I like when they do that," he says. "I like strong women."

—

Karla is one of the few regulars (maybe the only one, in fact) who actually buys stuff whenever she visits my shop. She'll buy $20 or $30 worth of books at a time. She doesn't own a TV and lives alone with her seven dogs. She started coming into my shop last summer when she discovered my collection of Terry Pratchett books, none of which I had read and probably never will now since she bought every single one.

Karla is planning a move out to New Mexico. She has lived in Dallas most of her life. She remembers when the area around Greenville Avenue was mostly farmland. She also remembers happening upon the body of a black man that had been hanged from a tree. She'd been out riding horses that day with a group of schoolchildren. She says she saw the man's body silhouetted in the distance as she crested a hill.

My buddy Joe, another of my flea market regulars, told me a similar story. I asked him if things were worse now than they were back then, considering all the bullshit with politics, Democrats versus Republicans, liberals versus conservatives, blacks versus whites, the hatred and vitriol stoked by 24/7 cable news TV, the constant paranoia, and fear- and hate-mongering.

No comparison, he said. His family relocated from Chicago to Dallas when he was a teenager. He's sixty-seven now. He remembers the first time his family took a roadtrip through the South. You'd see bodies hanging from the overpasses and trees, he told me. His mother told him not to look, but he couldn't help not looking. "Oh, no. Things are a lot better now," he says.

Karla is tired of Dallas. She says she's had it with Republicans and their ideologies. If you ask her, it's worse now than it was back then. Plus, she tells me, she's getting old. She's in her seventies now and has a difficult time driving at night. Night blindness, she explains. She wants to get out to New Mexico where her real friends are and where she truly feels at home. "You know what they do out there?" she says. "They have this thing where they all go out in the evening and watch the sun set. Nothing else. They just watch the sunset, and honey, it's such a wonderful and beautiful thing."

She tried explaining this to the guys she works with at UPS, but none of them could understand what the big deal was with watching the sunset.

She throws her hands up in exasperation. "I gotta get outta here."

—

This year has been one long ass-kicking beatdown. And it ain't over yet. 26 more days to go. Although I do suspect this season of change does not strictly adhere to the calendar year. Perhaps other forces are at work -- the alignment of the planets, the mood of the people, one's karmic obligations, and so on -- too many millions of seemingly meaningless and unrelated data points to predict such occurrences with any accuracy but you damn well know when you're in the midst of it, these seasons of change.

—

"You will need to prove to me that you can do the work."
"I've been doing this for too long. I don't feel a need to prove myself to anyone anymore. I've grown beyond that point."

116

Just another one of the many conversations in my head. Things I felt like saying. Things I wish I had said. And actually ended up saying. I am the architect of my own demise.

I feel as if I am being constantly poked and prodded. Do this. Do that. Are you done? Are you there? Don't forget this, don't forget that. Not merely work-related, either. EVERYTHING -- wife, kid, house, bills, appointments -- EVERYTHING.

That two-week trip to Maui and Oahu last summer did little except to remind us how painful it can be to have to come home and face reality, however unexpected that reality became. I sensed a change in the air when we had to put our pet dachshund down last February after she had ruptured a disk in her back. That was the turning point heralding another season of change.

Oh, but to lay floating on my back once again in the warm blue waters of the Pacific Ocean, drifting like seaweed, just flowing with the tide.

—

Feeling confused, lost, completely obsolete. My so-called career as a software test engineer appears to be coming to an end. Twelve years' experience working in the industry, none of it relevant in today's job market. Obsolete, woefully obsolete.

I suppose I could stay current with my skill-sets. Learn what needs to be learned. Become fluent with new programming languages and industry buzzwords -- Java, Agile, cloud computing, collaboration, blah blah blah, whatever. The fact is, I'm not as interested in technology as I was twenty years ago. My interests, strangely enough, have brought me back full circle to writing with manual typewriters, publishing zines, and formulating plans to travel the world. I spend much time daydreaming about living in tiny places and working throwaway jobs that don't use up too much of my time or psyche. Working in the tech industry is none of that. It's hyper-competitive, and as is too often the case now, I find myself competing needlessly with the best and brightest from India and China. Supposedly, anyway. Most of it is backstabbing egomania. Cockroaches stepping over each other, crawling up each other's asses trying to survive. I don't care. I've worked with my share of dumbfucks and morons from all over the globe. The petty, small-minded behavior doesn't faze me anymore. The Third World mindset is all about getting to the cheese no matter what the cost. Buddha? Gandhi? Who the hell were they? They were not capitalists. Their sole ambition was to help others. You can't make any money off of that.

Learning cool new things is cool, until you find yourself stuck in the infinite churn of a six-month release cycle. Then it begins to feel like a lot of pointless wheel-spinning in the mud, churning the same old bullshit over and over again. It sucks the life out of you. You awake after fifteen, twenty years and realize: Holy shit. Another generation lost.

Sure, maybe the pay is good compared to the risk, but sitting hunched over a keyboard and staring at a monitor all day isn't the most physically demanding activity. Workplace hazards can include tendonitis, carpal tunnel syndrome, pot belly, poor blood circulation, lower back pain, neck pain. Compare and contrast with the guys fixing roofs or doing yardwork for a living. I would offer that twenty-plus years of relative inactivity is worse for the mind and body than jobs that require bending, stooping, climbing, or working outdoors.

Me, I like driving aimlessly around town; walking around; exploring new neighborhoods; hanging out at the flea market and chatting with customers, even if most of them never buy a thing from my shop. No pressure, no stress, the sort of living which requires little more than allowing myself to become a part of the flow of life and enjoying it while I can. There is little room for Type-A personalities or middle-manager douchebags sending out email invitations to endless meetings to talk about pointless deadlines. Who cares? I don't. I don't think I ever did.

Looking into becoming an over-the-road truck driver. Sent in applications to a few trucking companies -- Swift, Schneider, Stevens Transport -- going to see about training/schooling to obtain my Class A commercial driver's license. Watched a bunch of Youtube videos uploaded by over-the-road truck drivers -- "Your Boy E the Trucker," "Trucker Josh and Diesel." A bunch of them regularly post videos. I've seen enough to get an idea of the life. The pay is low -- your first year out you probably won't make more than $20k or $40k, and you top out around $50k to $70k once you've put some miles and years under your belt.

The job is dangerous -- icy roads, snow storms, morning commutes, accidents on the highway, breakdowns in the middle of the night in the middle of nowhere.

So....low pay and one of the most dangerous jobs. Additionally, you will spend many long weeks on the road away from home. It's what they call a "lifestyle" occupation. You don't just do it. You live it.

Why do I want to do it? Like others have said before and more eloquently -- it is the call of the open road. It is the notion of living the nomad's life, always on the go. No time to hang around, nice to meet you, thank you very much, gotta get moving. Time for me to GO.

No boss to deal with. No office politics or egomaniacs. No dealing with other people's bullshit. Sure, you'll probably encounter assholes on the road, but at least you won't have to see them on a daily basis. Don't like someone? Don't get along? Move on. No need to involve human resources. No need to "work through differences." At the end of the day you're going to go home and realize that nobody really gives a shit what you think or how you feel. Everyone else is busy trying to survive themselves. So head out onto the open road and go it alone.

Trip Notes: Mexico City/Costa Rica

(I accepted an offer to work at Capital One as a "cloud engineer" on their production support team, but before I submitted my two-week notice at my current company, I decided to take a trip somewhere and use up all of my vacation time. So I traveled to Mexico and Costa Rica in July 2016. I visited Mexico City for a few days before flying to San Jose, Costa Rica.)

—

Mexico City, Mexico:

I arrived in Mexico City at 10:30pm on a Monday night and caught a taxi to my hotel. The driver learned that I was from the U.S. and began speaking to me in English. He was thankful, he said, that he had another opportunity to practice the language. A woman from California was his language teacher. He'd known her for 20 years. His English contained no discernible accent. I might as well have been conversing with someone back in the States. This was something I noticed with quite a number of people I interacted with while I was in Mexico City who were kind enough to speak English with this non-Spanish speaking Americano -- their English sounded like American English. I could hear no "Mexican" accent.

I spent that first night at the Marquis Reforma, a swanky place along Avenida Reforma in the heart of the financial district. This was the most "well-appointed" room I stayed at during my entire trip -- mini-bar, peanuts, assorted candies, condoms, toothpaste, perfumed soap, a bite-sized Hershey's chocolate bar on the pillow, fluffy white pillows and virgin-white bed sheets, 24-hour room service, glass shower with two shower heads. I got carried away and drank a shot of Jack Daniels. Then chased it down with four beers. One o'clock in the morning found me eating a hamburger that tasted as if it had been reheated in a microwave. I was hungry, though, and maybe a little drunk and didn't complain. Queasy and hungover the next morning, I vomited in the bathroom sink with the granite counter tops and tried to sleep it off until my 11am check-out time.

In the lobby, business people in suits gave me looks as I checked out with my wheeled suitcase whose underside I had spray-painted a bright green color (for easy identification at baggage claim). This is the sort of hotel for visiting foreign dignitaries and diplomats -- chandeliers, polished marble, bellhops hurrying to assist with your luggage, fancy-looking people in fancy-looking clothes. Not my kind of place. I asked the desk clerk how much it would cost to stay until Thursday, which is when I was scheduled to fly out to Costa Rica. He informed me that I had gotten a discount ($60US/night) when I originally booked the room online, but he would have to raise the rate to $222US per night going forward. I thanked him and left. Good thing I booked a room in another hotel the night before. On Google Maps, this new place looked like an easy two or three blocks down Avenida Reforma and just around the corner. An easy fifteen-minute stroll. In reality, not every corner contains street signs, and the various roundabouts had me going in circles a few times. I spent an hour or so wandering around the Zona Rosa district trying to find the place.

—

One thing struck me immediately as I wandered along those calles and avenidas -- this doesn't seem to be a place geared for the tourist industry. Mexico City is sophisticated. Cosmopolitan. This is no rinky-dink south-of-the-border town, nor was it some touristy beach spot riddled with sunburned vacationers looking for a tour guide. Many people I passed on the sidewalks appeared to be professionals sharply dressed in business suits, carrying briefcases, hurrying to office jobs. Rush-hour on a Tuesday morning in Mexico City, and there I was woefully under-dressed, pulling along my green spray-painted suitcase, weaving through the crowds, peeking up at the sun peeking back at me through gaps in the high-rise buildings. There are no street hawkers pressing tour pamphlets into your hand. There are no souvenir shops selling snow globes or t-shirts. There were no double-decker tour buses with some guy calling out landmarks and other points of interest on a loudspeaker. There were very few tourists, in fact, and that was fine with me. I was the only guy wearing a baseball cap and sneakers, it seemed, in a sea of business suits and leather attaches.

—

It's shameful what passes for Japanese cuisine in Mexico City.

On my second evening, I ate at a Japanese restaurant. It seemed like a high-end place -- packed with more people in business suits. The facade was designed like a Japanese teahouse with fake koi pond just inside the entrance. Up a winding, narrow flight of stairs was the seating area. The menus were fancy. That's about all I can say about the place. The food tasted as if it had been prepared by someone who only had Japanese cuisine described to him and had never actually eaten it himself. The teriyaki steak was cooked in a stir-fry fashion using thin strips and then covered with soy sauce instead of actual teriyaki sauce. The California rolls appeared to be macaroni salad wrapped in seaweed. Maybe I should have ordered the udon.

I spent the rest of the evening wandering around the Zona Rosa district, wondering why I didn't eat at that pizzeria I had passed earlier in the day. It smelled good and was packed with a lunchtime crowd of businessmen and young couples huddled around tiny tables. Which is what big cities are for -- business and romance. You don't go to New York City to go grocery shopping at Walmart, and you don't travel to San Francisco to get your tires rotated (at least not in the literal sense). And you certainly don't travel to Mexico City to eat at Japanese restaurants.

—

The next day I rode the subway to Bosque de Chapultepec. My hotel was around the corner from Insurgentes station, which is only two stops away. Like any other big city public transit system, the place is busy and bustling, people whizzing by me with their tickets. I got stuck at the turnstile. I wasn't sure if I was supposed to hand the ticket to the guard who was standing next to it or if I needed to scan it across the red light. The latter failed with the guard watching me patiently, so I handed it to her. She smiled and demonstrated passing the ticket through the slot. Like in any other subway system. Duh.

Downstairs underground, I weaved through another wave of people that had just been deposited by the train now departing. I had my digital camera out and took a few pictures. Then I switched to video mode and began recording. I noticed people giving me looks. In the distance, two uniformed police officers were watching me. I smiled and waved at them, then began recording a view of the subway tunnel. One of them began shouting at me. I don't speak Spanish, but I could tell from the tone and alarm in their voice that they wanted me to stop filming. I shut off the camera and slipped it back into my pack, but they motioned me to take it back out. They wanted me to delete any photos or video I had taken of the subway, which I did with both of them staring closely at the camera's tiny screen. When they were sure every last one was deleted, they smiled and let me go.

There is a red line which demarcates the last train on the platform. I stood there waiting to board, but one of the officers shook his head and waved me toward the front of the platform. "Woman," he said pointing at the red line on the ground, "woman." Ah, only women and children are allowed to ride in the last train. I nodded and he smiled.

—

Bosque de Chapultepec. I like saying "Bosque de Chapultepec."

The name was a relic from my junior high school years. All I knew about Bosque de Chapultepec was whatever I had read in old textbooks containing faded photographs of worn-out looking people in outdated clothing. Now here I was, some thirty-five years later walking around the place. Bosque de Chapultepec. It wasn't on my list of Top 100 Places I Need to Visit Before I Die. It wasn't even on my list of places to visit during this trip. I had a five-hour layover in Mexico City on my way to Costa Rica and decided to stay a few extra days instead.

I strolled along the promenade as vendors prepared to open their little shopping booths for the day. I bought a few t-shirts for the wife and kid. Besides the gift shops at the airport, this was the only place that had anything resembling touristy t-shirts and souvenir tchotchkes. I continued onward to the museum of natural history, enjoying the peace and calm -- a nice respite from the hectic sidewalk hustle and bustle of the financial district.

The museum was okay. I've never really cared much for looking at little clay model "depictions" of what life must have been like back in the day, much of it seeming dry, lifeless, and probably inaccurate. Where is all the life? Laughter? Spiritual hallucinatory visions into higher dimensional realms? Probably in another museum. Outside were a few replicas of ancient Mayan pyramids. Why not use the real thing? Then I remembered -- our highly advanced, technological society lacks the expertise to transport large one-ton blocks of stone over great distances and hoist them into place with such precision that even now, centuries later, it is not possible to slip a piece of paper between any two blocks. But we'll charge you admission to see a replica of such a thing.

Wandering around this place gave me the perfect excuse to do just that -- wander around for a few hours. I took more notice of the other museum visitors, many of whom seemed to be tourists from other Latin American countries. They were well-dressed and obviously possessed the sort of lifestyle that allowed them to take vacations and spend money in places like this Museum of Natural History. These were not the same Mexicans trying to sneak across the border into the United States.

Afterward, I took another stroll through the rest of the park. The air seemed so much fresher and cleaner amidst the trees lining the walkways. Squirrels ventured close, unafraid and curious. Butterflies fluttered about. Couples paired-off on benches in the shade, snuggling and kissing -- such public displays of affection rarely seen back in the States. I sat on a bench alone and collected some soil in a plastic bag. A keepsake souvenir of sorts, a reminder of a peaceful time spent in a city I had never meant to visit.

On the way back -- I walked instead of taking the subway -- I ate at a food cart in the financial district. Ten pesos for a gordita. It was delicious.

—

San Jose, Costa Rica:

I made the flight to San Jose after very nearly being booted off on account of the fact that the airline had overbooked it. I was the last guy to board and found myself sitting between two Hispanic women -- an attractive young woman at the window seat and an older matronly woman on the aisle. On a few occasions, I caught the older woman glaring at the younger one with a look of anger and disdain; I thought maybe they knew each other. A flight attendant came by handing out slips of paper, government documentation for us to fill out -- passport numbers, name, address, etc. The older woman held a Costa Rican passport. The younger one was a Mexican native. I surmised the younger one was a working gal flying into Costa Rica for the weekend to ply her trade -- she was traveling alone with two iPhones and only a small carry-on. I gathered the older woman, a matronly tica, did not approve. Detective work complete, I fell asleep in my seat, my head periodically bobbing forward and jolting me awake.

Arriving in Costa Rica, known for being a touristy destination, I expected the airport to be more crowded, like Honolulu or Cancun, but the place was empty. Perhaps I had arrived during the off-season? Maybe people were afraid of the zika virus? It was 10:30 in the morning. I wasn't complaining; I just found it curious. The customs official sleepily waved everyone through. I'm not even sure his X-ray machine was turned on.

—

124

I needed cash for the cab ride into San Jose. The clerk at the money exchange counter said it would cost about 20,000 colons -- "or around $30US." Currency conversion would be an annoyance throughout my stay in Costa Rica. The difference in the cost of various things was exponential:

500 colons for a bag of peanuts.

2,400 colons for the bus ride to Jaco.

6,000 colons for a plate of eggs with beans and rice.

17,000 colons for a fried fish dinner at a fancy hotel restaurant.

I grew tired of sifting through crumpled bills fished out of my pocket and resorted to paying for everything with a credit card whenever possible.

—

It was a thirty-minute drive into San Jose from the airport. The rust-stained buildings and encroaching tropical greenery reminded me of driving down the H1 through Honolulu on the way to Waikiki. The taxi driver -- a kid who couldn't have been more than twenty -- expertly shifted and down-shifted gears on that Toyota mini-bus. I grew a little jealous, having been reminded of my own ineptitude at shifting through the gear pattern while learning to drive a big-rig Freightliner with a 10-speed Eaton Fuller manual transmission. I sucked at it.

I checked into the Hotel Colonial on *Calle 11*, between *Avenidas 2* and *6*. "Writer's garret" was the first thing that came to mind upon entering my room, perhaps not an entirely accurate description -- "garret" denotes a cramped or dismal place -- but I was thinking of the word more in the sense of a cozy little hideaway with a good sized writing desk and adequate lighting -- the sort of place to hunker down and write the great Central American novel. The rooms (at least the ones I stayed in -- #27 and #28) were accented with dark wood throughout -- dark wooden floors that creaked when you walked upon them, large wooden armoire, and a sturdy wooden writing desk. Each room was furnished with an extremely soft and comfortable bed, a ceiling fan, and an air-conditioning unit. I could stay here for a month instead of the three days I had reserved, but I decided to make my way to Jaco sooner rather than later and checked out after the second night.

An attractive woman at the front desk pointed out the main shopping area on a little tourist map she gave me -- Central Avenue or *Avenida Central*, which is about a ten-block stretch of shops and restaurants, and random street performers. There's even a Starbucks's and a McDonald's. I spent most of my time wandering around this area while I was in San Jose. It gets a little sketchy if you go a few blocks north in some areas. You start seeing the drug addicts, junkies, and prostitutes; mental cases screaming at lamp posts; people staggering about with bloodshot eyes, obviously high on some kind of manufactured substance. Reminded me of the decade I spent living in San Francisco's Tenderloin district. Here in San Jose, there are police on many corners standing around looking bored, though they are unarmed and appear as poor and desperate as the rest of them.

—

I'm glad I brought along my laptop for this trip. I didn't book every room in advance, so I had to spend some time figuring out where I was going to be sleeping for certain portions of my visit. Just like a real traveler. It's so much easier looking at maps and hotel listings on a 15-inch computer screen. Is it worth lugging around that extra weight? Maybe. I suppose it's a matter of personal preference. I had brought along a 40-liter "tactical" backpack and a rolling suitcase. I wasn't exactly traveling light this time around. There were a number of things I never used and probably should have left behind: military desert combat boots, binoculars, GPS device, twice the number of socks and underwear than I actually used -- all the things I thought I'd need if I found myself lost and alone in the Costa Rican jungle. Truth is, I never ventured more than a mile beyond an asphalt road with cab drivers in little red cars waiting for me to hail them at any time for a ride back to the hotel. My rolling suitcase was overloaded with t-shirts and souvenirs for the wife and kid.

While searching for hotels, I kept the TV tuned to Telehit, the Latin American equivalent of MTV, if MTV had continued playing music videos. This became a kind of ritual for me as I checked into various rooms and continued even to my next trip along the Caribbean coast of Mexico -- one of the first things I did after setting my bag upon the bed was to turn on the TV and find the channel that had Telehit. If there was a nuclear attack just outside my window; if the natives were in revolt and setting cars and trash cans on fire; if the Pacific Ocean rose up and submerged the entire town; it didn't matter -- as long as Telehit was playing on my hotel TV everything seemed okay. It was like listening to Sunday morning Christian radio on the drive out to east Texas. Some things just seemed to fit.

According to Google Maps, Jaco is the nearest beach town from San Jose -- only an hour or so away and reachable by bus. I checked out of my room and caught a little red taxi to the bus station. It's known as Terminal 7-10, named I presume for the fact that the station is located on the corner of Avenida 7 and Calle 10. Although the terminal building itself is nice and relatively safe, multi-leveled, well-lighted and air-conditioned, the surrounding area can be a little sketchy -- lots of drug addicts and homeless looking people wandering about. One-way tickets to Jaco run about $1,700 colones. Tickets can be purchased on the second level, right above where passengers wait for the buses at street level. Unlike buses in the U.S., seats are assigned. Your seat assignment will be listed on the ticket. Also important to keep in mind: There is no air-conditioning or toilets on these buses. So do your thing before you leave.

—

I wasn't planning anything too exciting or strenuous. Simply wandering about was the point of my adventure. My goal wasn't to fill every day with the sort of activities you find in travel brochures or on tourist websites, things that require tour guides taking you on jungle treks or zip-lining through the forest canopy. I wanted to soak in the experience of simply being in the place. Find a beach, sit around, and daydream for a while -- basically spend some time doing a whole lot of nothing. It would have been nice to go strolling through the jungle, but I prefer to do that at my own pace and at my own leisure. I didn't want to spend money on a rental car, and the jungle was too far away -- although I could see it in the distance and the bus taking us to Jaco through those windy highway roads brushed right up against the edge of it, the jungle was beyond walking distance. For now the jungle waited, hovering like a shadow along the edges of a dream. Next time perhaps.

—

Jaco is a messy little beach town. There is one main road leading in and out of the jungle. Touristy restaurants, shops and hotels line either side. You see the usual beach town beach bums hanging around, pedaling beach-cruisers or carrying surfboards. The skies were overcast when I arrived and remained that way the duration of my stay. The gloom contrasted with this seeming laid-back beach vacation getaway. Dark clouds hovered near the horizon, a foreboding doom in the distance. I took my lunch at a small pizza place on the northern end of the main street. A young woman peeked from behind her station at the pizza oven while I placed my order with a guy who I assumed was her brother. She smiled and waved at me. When I left, glancing over my shoulder, I saw that she was still smiling and waving. I thanked her and smiled back. Walking back to my room I wondered if she was hoping to meet someone who could save her from that pizza parlor life in that messy little beach town with dark clouds and shadowy waves.

—

My room at the Hotel Mar de Luz was large and gloomy. The two queen-size beds were swallowed by the room; there was still room enough to fit at least another. The lone bulb in the ceiling high above only illuminated the rafters and made the dark wooden walls seem darker. Another excellent room in which to write the great Central American novel. If it had a writing desk. I had to set my laptop atop the small refrigerator in order to use it. I tuned the TV to Telehit and all my paranoid concerns melted away into sugary-pop pointlessness. I headed out to find the beach.

Very few tourists were out and about. Maybe it was the off-season. Locals were camped in rusty vehicles in the parking lot and on the beach itself in a few spots. The ocean mimicked the sky and carried a foreboding pall, its dark waves lapping a shadowy red sand beach. Here, Mother Nature seemed unwelcoming and sinister. And always looming in the distance, the jungle. Low-tide with the shore far off and away, I strolled along the beach, side-stepping beer cans and plastic bags. A middle-aged white guy, pot-bellied and hopeful, passed me with a surfboard under his arm. A while later I spotted him in the distance trying to realize his surfing fantasies on knee-high waves.

—

Dinner that first night was rotisserie chicken. I ordered two pieces of chicken and took a seat at one of the plastic tables beneath the fan. It was muggy and warm. I learned soon enough that not too many places in Jaco possess air-conditioning. I saw the guy take two whole chickens from the roaster and I got up to clarify that I only wanted two pieces. I'd had a similar problem a day earlier at a fried chicken place run by a Chinese family back in San Jose. The girl working the counter glared disdainfully when I asked in Spanish if she spoke English. When I tried to order two pieces of chicken, she shouted something in Chinese to her brother who returned with two whole chickens. I tried to clarify that I only wanted two pieces of chicken. She pretended not to understand and tried to ring me up for two whole chickens. We went back and forth for a few minutes, and she began berating me in Spanish. Then she turned to a well-dressed Hispanic man who was waiting in line behind me and said something else in Spanish. I watched him shrug and shake his head as she smirked in some kind of Chinese-immigrant-who-speaks-fluent-Spanish superiority. The matter was resolved when one of the busboys, an older Costa Rican woman, offered to translate for me.

"Ah, dos piezas," she said.

"Si, si, si," I said, "Gracias!"

The Chinese girl, filled with hatred and contempt, tossed my plate of chicken at me from across the counter.

Fortunately, the family-run place in Jaco treated me with much better respect. The woman laughed, apologizing in Spanish. I ate my two-piece fried chicken meal while fending off a curious bee, which is another thing I came to realize about Jaco -- instead of flies, there are bees. Every outdoor meal I ate meant having to contend with a bee or two buzzing about my plate. They weren't aggressive, but I also didn't want to get stung and was as gentle as possible when shooing them away.

Also, restaurants here like to serve everything with a bottle of ketchup. Chicken, pizza, fried fish. Doesn't matter. That bottle of ketchup is placed right there next to your plate. Ketchup, bees, and one flimsy napkin.

—

I spent my mornings wandering along the beach. When I began to feel too warm and muggy, I'd dip into the ocean, then sit for a bit on the sand, watching the dark waves roll in. It seemed very prehistoric, as if at any moment I'd spot a plesiosaur breaking the surface with a seal in its mouth, or pterodactyls fluttering in the distance, ducking into the shadows of the murky jungle. I spent the afternoon hours in my room, napping and reading Paul Theroux's 'The Happy Isles of Oceania.'

There wasn't much else to see in this town, and I wondered how the locals could stand it, day after day, year after year. Everything has to be trucked in, except the ocean and the jungle. All those bottles of Heinz Ketchup and cases of Corona. Someone must be buying it. I caught the bus back to San Jose after a few days. I hung around for another few days, took in a few of the museums as I had been meaning to do, then caught the flight home.

Pura vida!

—

Trip Notes:
- 15" Dell laptop (never leave home without it. came in handy for researching hotels and searching Google Maps)
- Samsung Galaxy S4 cell phone (Skyping with wife and kid. Backup for taking pictures and video.)
- Canon PowerShot ELPH-180 (broke it when I dropped it onto the tile floor in the hotel in Jaco)
- Bluetooth keyboard (used once while drinking coffee at the Starbuck's in San Jose.)
- Binoculars (never used)
- GPS handheld device (never used)

Note on getting through customs in Mexico:

When you arrive in Mexico, the flight attendants will hand out a green immigration form for you to complete. (By default, they will hand you a form printed in Spanish, but English ones are available if you ask for one.) You will need to present this form to Mexican customs officials before they allow you into the baggage claim area when you arrive at the airport. The customs agent will stamp this form as well as your passport. Be sure to keep the immigration form with your passport. You'll need to present it to the gate agent when you leave the country on your flight out.

This nearly caused me to get bumped from the flight from Mexico to Costa Rica. When I went to check-in my luggage at the AeroMexico counter, the agent asked me for the form and at that particular moment -- it was six in the morning and I was half asleep -- I didn't know what she was talking about and said I didn't have it. (I realized later that the form was in my backpack mixed in with miscellaneous receipts and other scraps of paper). She proceeded to check my suitcase and wrote "Pending immigration form" on my boarding pass.

At the gate, I realized I hadn't been assigned a seat number. The gate agent took my boarding pass and said to give him a few minutes. Minutes went by and then it was boarding time and everyone got onto the plane except me. I reminded the gate agent that I had found my immigration form and waved it politely in front of his face. He smiled, "Un momento." I stood there in the near empty terminal watching the other gate agents shut the doors and begin shutting down until the next flight.

"My bag is on that plane," I said. He smiled, "Un momento."

Turned out the flight had been overbooked, but luckily for me a family of three failed to show up and I was allowed onto the flight. I think if I had shown that immigration form to the agent earlier that morning I would have been guaranteed a seat and wouldn't have had to experience that last-minute near panic feeling of being booted from a flight. Better yet, I should have utilized that 24-hour web check-in feature on AeroMexico's website and selected my own seat online, which is exactly what I did for my flight home a week later.

10-day trip: July 11, 2016 to July 21, 2016
Hotels I stayed at:
- Mexico City, Mexico:
  Marquis Reforma Hotel Spa
  Hotel Royal Reforma
- San Jose, Costa Rica:
  Hotel Colonial
  Hemingway Inn
- Jaco, Costa Rica:
  Hotel Mar de Luz

Total cost of the entire trip: I have no idea. I put it all on a credit card. I estimated I spent between two to four thousand dollars total. I'll know for sure when I receive the bill. Reckless, I know, but sometimes you gotta live.

Trip Notes: Cancun/Playa Del Carmen
(November 2016)

That gig at Capital One didn't pan out. I had originally signed on to work as a "scripting engineer," of which my primary responsibility would be writing software to automate tasks performed in "the cloud," but I instead found myself working a graveyard shift on a 24/7 support team performing entry-level level production support, key points that they somehow failed to mention in the job description or during the interview. We were approaching the holidays (it was early November), and I said to Waseem, a coworker with nearly thirty year's tech experience under his belt, "What the hell are we doing here? It's two in the morning and we're clicking links on websites."

"We have to pay the bills," he said. Waseem immigrated from Pakistan in the 80's and spent much of the last decade living in Mississippi. He recently bought a house out here in North Texas. One of those $400k McMansions. He was nearing sixty.

"I don't think I'll make it to Christmas. This is bullshit."

"C'mon, man," he says, "We just started working here. It's not that bad, really."

"That's what prisoners tell themselves when they've been in prison for too long."

I spent much of the time wandering around each floor in the six buildings. I was like a ghost in the middle of the night, spying people's personal belongings on their desks -- pictures of their families, little awards, and all the sort of miscellany people bring into their work environment to make them feel more at home. It was depressing, observing the sort of life I lived just a few years prior. Lifeless now, in shadow and stillness. In the middle of the night it was peaceful and quiet. Waseem and I would go for walks around the campus. Often we'd see bunny rabbits everywhere, their eyes reflecting in the lamplight. They were like furry zombies that crept out of the bushes when everyone else was asleep, creeping about in silence.

After three months, I decided I'd had enough. I submitted my resignation and booked the next flight to Mexico.

—

Cancun - Day 1 - 11/27/16 - Getting there:

Alarm went off at 4am. Nadjet and Sara were asleep in the living room. They agreed to stay at the house and watch the dogs while I was gone. Made a pot of coffee. Brushed my teeth. Then fretted over the fact that I would be traveling with two bags -- a Maxpedition Vulcan II pack and a Tumi satchel (I got the Maxpedition pack at an online sale for $80, and I found the Tumi bag at a thrift shop for $4). I pride myself on being a light traveler. And I always end up traveling with an overloaded backpack and an equally overloaded satchel -- way over-packed for a mere five-day trip, but it was too late to re-organize; the taxi to bring me to the airport had already been dispatched. I got to the airport at about 5:30am and breezed through the security checkpoint. It appears the TSA has done away with requiring passengers to remove their shoes or remove laptops from bags. This would not be the case on my return flight through Fort Lauderdale. I ate a bagel with cream cheese and washed it down with a cup of coffee.

During the flight, I sat next to two loud and chatty American women. I had them pegged as Arizona gun-nut conservatives. Facebook fake news blowhards. Post-truth Trump supporters. The antisocial loner in me was annoyed at first, but I soon discovered they were friendly and good-natured, regardless of whatever political leanings they favored.

I couldn't help but notice the younger one was amply-bosomed beneath a flimsy t-shirt as she gestured and spoke excitedly to her companion -- an aunt or older friend, I assumed. I overheard them discussing the younger one's struggles with anxiety and the various men in her life. It seems she was on her way to meet another guy who ran a bar or nightclub somewhere. The younger one, they explained to me, was relocating to Playa del Carmen to begin a new life. She had grown tired of living in the United States and had recently spent nine months living in a small Mexican town in the mountains. "I need to get away from the States for a while. People are too stressed out. There's too much -- " She clenched her fists.

"Politics?" I said.

"Yes!" said the younger one, "I need to be alone for a little while." The older woman nodded knowingly.

—

Our plane touched down at 10:30am, and I caught a taxi into *el centro*. It cost the usual three-hundred and something pesos (about $30US) that I paid to the lady behind the glass window at the taxi counter. The ride into town flooded my mind with memories of all the years we had traveled here as a family. Sara was in the third or fourth grade when we vacationed in Cancun for the first time back in 2009. We have a photo on the wall of her playing on the beach with her plastic shovel and bucket on the beach near the Fiesta Americana. I asked her recently how her friend Mackenzie was doing. "That was my friend from second grade, Dad," she said, "I'm in high school now." The years just slipped away.

—

I checked into room 230 at the Adhara Hacienda (formerly known as the Radisson Hacienda). Besides the change of name, the place looks exactly the same. The 15-passenger van was out front waiting to take another group of tourists to the Hotel Zone. I recognized just one of the bellhops from previous years; the others must have moved onto other things. Construction workers were busy setting up scaffolding in the center of the lobby area. This is where they would be installing a sixteen-foot Christmas tree, gaudy and all-white. One of the few reminders that we had officially entered the holiday season. It didn't feel like Christmas to me.

—

I caught a cab to the Hotel Zone, hoping to eat a slice of pizza before jumping into the ocean, but it was Sunday morning and many places were still closed. A place called Carlos 'N Charlie's was the only place that was open. We'd eaten here before. Typical overpriced tourist fare with the waiters doing idiotic tricks like balancing drinks on their heads as they brought them to the table, which is what my waiter did. I was the only one in the restaurant. I just wanted something to eat -- I wasn't looking for that Cancun Spring Break experience, but I congratulated him anyway and proceeded to wait for my tacos (or enchiladas or something) for the next half hour. The food was forgettable but enough to tide me over. The waiter returned with my check a short while later, saying: "Tips are a mandatory fifty-percent." What? Was I paying for that balancing trick with the beer on his head? I didn't know if he was joking; he wasn't smiling when he said it. I shrugged; the total bill, including this usurious tip, worked out to about $24US. The kid probably needed it more than I did. Whatever -- I'll never eat there again.

The walkway to the beach led me past Club Coco Bongo -- the wife and I always laughed whenever we saw that sign because it reminded us of Coco, our dearly departed dachshund. Sunday morning and the beach wasn't too crowded, although a DJ was trying to get people stirred up. I hurried past the throngs of white beach chairs and annoying hip-hop music. Further down the beach, I was greeted with blue skies and blue, blue water. Even here in tourist central, at its most garish and banal, the Caribbean sea asserts her beauty. I admire her from a distance, briefly dipping into the warm and soothing waters along the shore. This is what was calling out to me while I worked that graveyard shift at Capital One. Now I lay floating on my back in the warm water with a Caribbean sun on my face.

In the distance I heard a whistle. Or was it sea birds clamoring for fast-food leftovers from tourists? I was content to remain floating along the surface. But the whistling persisted. I craned my head up and saw a lifeguard blowing his whistle and waving his arms. He waited for me to get out of the water and said I couldn't swim where I'd been swimming. There was a dangerous riptide, he said. Then he instructed me to swim a few hundred yards up the shore where the crowd was and where the DJ was playing his music, which made no sense to me. Instead I rested on the sand where I was and went back into the water when the lifeguard went away. I wondered why there weren't many people over on this side -- the water here was the same as the water a few hundred yards in the other direction. A short while later I watched as a hotel attendant indicated something similar to a Mexican family whose kids were splashing around near the shore in front of me. When I left I spotted a sign sitting crooked in the sand, "Privado...," and noticed the fancy condos behind me. Perhaps residents were tired of drunken tourists ruining their view? Although technically designated by the Mexican government as being public property, the reality is that the beaches in the Hotel Zone are controlled by the hotels that front them, and they hire attendants to shoo away anyone who isn't a registered guest. I've only encountered this annoyance in Cancun, and maybe that's why vacationers have started going elsewhere.

I walked to another beach toward the northern end of the strip and swam in the shadow of a hotel with the locals near a rotting pier.

—

I'm spending the next five days in Mexico. Here as in any other beach town, I am reminded of a universal truth: the ocean is the great equalizer, and the beach is where she comes to play with her human visitors. Politics, financial status, or social standing have little influence here. I watch from my spot on the sand as waves knock around old men and laughing children alike. The ocean forces you to be playful and to take part in this joyous existence called life. There is little to fear except your own inhibitions.

Dinner that first night was at a place called La Parrilla near Mercado 28 in El Centro. There was some kind of soccer match playing on the TV, and men were craning their heads and moving tables to get a good look at the action. Their spouses and girlfriends feigned interest then returned to their meals. Here, too, yet another circus act -- a diminutive waiter balanced large bowl-like glasses of beer on his head as he delivered them to each table. He appeared to be in his fifties or sixties. Surely he must be sick of all the tourists laughing and gawking at him. Late at night, when his shift is over, I imagine he returns to a tiny concrete hovel, perhaps somewhere here in the same neighborhood, and goes to sleep alone on a mat on the bare floor. Late morning the next day, he awakes to do it all over again. He can't remember the last time he's seen the ocean or been to the beach. He has one day off and that day is spent shopping for groceries or trying to find a dentist to fix his rotting teeth. No time for la playa. He might have five kids and a spouse somewhere or he might have none. The lives of the working poor can tell many variations of the same sad story.

The food at La Parrilla was okay, but I've had better Mexican cuisine back home in Dallas. Except for that place on Isla Mujeres where you can have two freshly-caught lobsters for about $27US, the food in Cancun is never really that great. But at least there was no mandatory fifty-percent tip.

—

Cancun - Day 2 - 11/28/2016:
One of my favorite things in Cancun is the breakfast at *Los Bisquets Obregon* (or *Los Bisquets Bisquets,* as I call it because that's how it's printed on their menu). I always order the *huevos con chorizo* (eggs with sausage). They serve it with a side cup filled with peppers and sliced vegetables marinated in pepper juices. Eat it with the fresh bread they bring in little baskets and wash it all down with hot coffee. It's like a Mexican Denny's, except cleanlier and less depressing.

It's a mostly locals restaurant -- many customers appear to be white-collar office worker types. Older couples humbly dressed in professional attire -- the men wearing pressed white shirts, dark slacks and the women in polyester business skirts and blouses disguising cleavage. I've remarked before about the public displays of affection the Mexican people exhibit toward their significant others -- holding hands, snuggling, tilting the head to one side while gazing into each other's eyes, a quick peck on the lips. You see this behavior with the school kids sitting at bus stops and with older couples seated in restaurants like Los Bisquets Bisquets. Mexicans are an affectionate people, unafraid to show love, something so basic yet sadly lacking in American culture, where everything is sex and porn, good guys versus bad guys, gun violence, pursed lips and fear of judgment from an angry Christian god. Is it any wonder we've become a nation of addicts wallowing in self-pity and resentment? The switch only goes from ON to OFF. There is no tuning dial which would allow us to gradually adjust our frequencies.

—

Mornings are when I like to go for walks and wander around the city, when the sun is still low and the weather hasn't grown unbearably muggy and warm. When you're only visiting a place one or two weeks at a time, it's difficult to acclimate to the environment. I envy the folks who can say they've vacationed at a certain spot for a month or two. I wish I had the freedom. Except for the water trucks and hotel workers on their way to their jobs, there are very few people about. The city is still asleep. It's also a good time to take a few pictures. The Caribbean sun casts everything in an orange glow.

I see water trucks delivering their supply to small boutique hotels and even a few larger ones. I'm disturbed to realize how many of these places rely on a water source that has to be trucked in. Do tourists realize they are one uprising away from slurping water from puddles like stray dogs wandering along abandoned streets? On Isla Mujeres one year, our hotel ran out of water the one night we were there. We had to wait for the water truck delivery in the morning. Fortunately, there was just a piddle enough dripping out of the faucet to allow us to sponge off the saltwater stickiness from playing at the beach all day. My wife was annoyed that she couldn't wash her hair. First World problems.

But what exactly do those water trucks indicate? Poor civic infrastructure, drought conditions, or both? Where is this water being trucked in from? I returned to my hotel, thankful for the bottled water in my room, got my backpack, and caught the ferry to Isla Mujeres.

I spent some time hiking along the coastline. Condominiums line the rocky shore overlooking the sea. Many are empty shells of buildings, lacking windows or doors, plastered with graffiti. 'For Sale' signs dot overgrown yards.

There are no man-made beaches on this side of the island -- it's lonelier, and the pounding surf provides a kind of tempo to my own quiet meditation and ponderings. My mind telescopes out across the years, and I begin to wonder where I went wrong with my marriage, my career. Everything. Random images flash through my mind, like old photos in a shoebox. Much of my life has been spent wandering alone in quiet observation. I'm okay with it. I am content and at peace.

—

The beach we've become so familiar with is no longer there. Literally, there is no more beach. Where there was sand five or six years ago has been reclaimed by the ocean. The shore goes right up to the restaurant/bar now. The hotels that made their business on renting beach chairs and providing lunch to beach-goers must now make do with a tenth of the beach front they once maintained. Ultimately, Mother Nature will be heard. Gaia makes her will known.

I spread out on one of the beach chairs and wait for my order of burgers and fries while drinking a beer. One of Mariah Carey's Christmas songs is playing at the bar, but it doesn't feel like Christmas on Isla Mujeres. Feels more like some kind of half-hearted paradise. I spend the rest of the afternoon lounging like an iguana in the sun. *Una mas cerveza, por favor*.

—

Weird dreams this afternoon. Took a quick nap when I returned to my hotel room. Didn't sleep for more than an hour or so. Dreamed I was back on the beach dozing in the beach chair when an extremely large shadow loomed out of the water. People began running. It was a huge alligator. I reminded myself that those things live in these parts. And typical in any dream of this kind, I was unable to move and struggled to get away. That was promptly followed by another dream where I was driving my van along what seemed like Legacy Ave. in Plano, near the Japanese restaurant where I always go for lunch. It was dark and the van started swerving on its own, as if something had taken control of it. It was night and pitch black out. No street lights or other cars were on the road. There was another passenger in the car -- a girl I didn't recognize. I told her to hang on because I was no longer in control of the van. Instead of being on Legacy, we were driving along a winding road near some cliffs. I tried to make a U-turn and the van stalled as I pulled over to the side of the road. It shut off, leaving us in pitch black darkness. I began saying to myself: "God is light. God is light." Then I awoke.

Dreams that feel real usually mean something. These dreams felt real. Hmm.

—

My last night in Cancun. Nightlife in El Centro is always somewhat sad and dark. There is a pavilion area, however, surrounded by food stalls and cotton candy carts that is always lively with families and music. Sometimes there's live entertainment. The wife and I were amazed to see families with young children out and about as late as nine or ten o'clock at night -- eating, laughing, playing. We'd remark to each other that back home in Plano, Texas people would be locking their doors by 6pm and in bed by 10pm. But now I'm here by myself. No reason to hang around.

I had dinner at a place called Altamar off Tulum Avenue -- enchiladas, chips and salsa, and a bottle of Pacifico. $130 pesos. The night's entertainment was a bat swooping out of the Christmas-light wrapped palm trees picking off insects.

On the way back to my hotel I passed a moping, depressed looking teen waiting at the bus stop. I composed a poem that I imagined singing to my daughter in Tejano style about the sad Mexican boy at the bus stop:

Lo siento, lo siento
I no dinero
(Chorus) No dinero!
She left me for a white boy from Plano
(Chorus) Plano!

—

Cancun/Playa del Carmen - Day 3 - 11/29/2016:
You can catch a jitney bus from Cancun's El Centro district to Playa del Carmen. You see them all over the place, going up and down Tulum Avenue. Little 15-passenger vans or mini-buses. I caught the one that has their stand across the parking lot from the ADO bus terminal. You'll hear the guy yelling, "La Playa! La Playa! La Playa!" Cost is $30 pesos. You can buy a ticket prior to departure, or you can just hop on and pay the driver upon arrival. It takes about

an hour to get to Playa del Carmen, where you are dropped off at a little bus terminal on Calle 2 Norte and 20 Ave. Norte. Head due east for five or six blocks and you'll hit the beach.

—

I had a room waiting for me at the Hotel Riviera Caribe Maya. According to the map on Expedia, it was just a few blocks north of Avenida Benito Juarez, a short five-minute walk from the bus depot. Expedia was wrong. After an hour of wandering up and down Avenida 10, I gave in and called the hotel for directions. Seems I hadn't wandered far enough. The hotel was about twenty blocks north of where I was. I complained about Expedia and how they needed to validate their map links. This could have a negative impact on revenue for the hotels who are paying to be a part of this online service. I was huffing and puffing and trying to find a spot in the shade to cool down. The lady on the phone was polite and in broken English suggested I take a cab. I walked instead and arrived a short while later, back drenched in sweat, tired and thirsty. Standing in front of a large electric fan in the lobby, I gave myself a few minutes to cool down before attempting to check-in. I didn't want to drip sweat all over the front desk. Minor inconveniences which pale in comparison to the rush of checking into a strange hotel in an unfamiliar city. Here I am with my backpack and satchel. This is all I have and perhaps this is all I'll ever need. I could live like this indefinitely. And people do, actually. They're posting YouTube videos and writing blogs all over the Internet. Me, I'm a short-timer, only here for the next three days. For now I'll just pretend and entertain fantasies of a carefree lifestyle. I dump my bags and head for the beach.

In the afternoon I wandered around town a bit. I found the Walmart but couldn't find any bars that weren't riddled with tourists and blaring music. Along the coastline, storms had washed away much of the beach front. Similar to what I had seen on Isla Mujeres, the water goes right up to the restaurants and bars in some places. This place is like Waikiki, except cheaper with less Asians.

My feet hurt. I haven't done this much walking since my trip to Mexico City and Costa Rica last July. I was planning to return to Cancun before my flight back home, but decided to spend my remaining time in Playa del Carmen. There is more life here and more places to eat. Cancun, it seems, has gone back to the locals -- quiet, low-key, very few restaurants.

I had dinner at a place called Sushi Ken on Avenida 10. (Sushi? In Mexico? Why not.) The place wasn't very crowded. Perhaps it was still early. I usually try to follow the traveler's rule of thumb when it comes to eating: If the place is crowded, the food is probably good. If the place is empty during the lunch time or dinner rush, the food probably sucks. But I was tired of walking and just wanted a quick bite to eat before heading back to the hotel. First sign of failure: I tried to order a beer. The waiter apologized and said they don't serve alcohol. Fair enough. Maybe they haven't been granted a liquor license yet. So I tried to order a few pieces of sushi -- maybe some unagi and yellow-fin tuna. The waiter again apologized and said I can only order ten pieces at a time. Okay, no problem. I ordered the combo roll. Glancing through the menu, the picture of miso ramen looked appetizing. Again, the traveler's rule of thumb -- never judge a dish by the photograph of it on the menu.

My meal arrived thirty minutes later -- a tepid bowl of miso soup with overcooked noodles thrown in and a few squares of seaweed layered over the top. The sushi combo roll tasted like it looked -- prepackaged supermarket sushi. Why didn't I learn from that last foray into Japanese cuisine in Mexico City? Oh well. $230 pesos.

—

Playa Del Carmen - Day 4 - 11/30/2016:
Last night I was awakened by a loud whooshing noise reverberating through the walls. In the morning when I tried to wash my face, there wasn't any water coming out of the bathroom faucet. That whooshing sound must have been the water draining out of the water tank on the hotel roof. Sure enough, on my way out through the lobby I passed a number of cleaning ladies mopping up water on the first floor. The girl at the front desk said the problem would be fixed in about two hours. My morning poop would not wait that long. I went into survival mode and hiked the fifteen minutes to Walmart. Expecting the worst, I was pleasantly surprised. The men's room was exceptionally clean and spacious, spotless in fact. Unlike the Walmart restrooms back in the States, there were no puddles of urine or clumps of toilet paper on the floor, no tracks of mud or homeless guys shuffling around mumbling to themselves, and there's always that one urinal that's continuously flushing. By comparison, Mexican Walmart was more like a stroll through a zen garden. Even the toilet paper dispensers were packed with fresh rolls of toilet paper. Of course, this could all be due to the fact that it was still

relatively early in the day. Definitely a more upscale public restroom experience.

Morning business complete, I walked south to Avenida Benito Juarez and headed west. I wanted to see what the local neighborhoods looked like on the other side of the freeway. The day was already warming up, everything bright and shimmery beneath a cloudless sky. I kept to the shadier side of the street. Morning rush-hour and traffic was headed downtown toward the beach. This part of Mexico must be considered upscale, perhaps even more so than Cancun. Although most everyone drives around those smaller compact cars -- they almost look like clown cars -- I spotted very few that were older than four or five years. My 2003 GMC Sonoma with its 250,000 miles would look horribly out of place here. Wealth everywhere, courtesy of the drug trade and tourism. Or so I imagined. What the hell do I know?

Walking along Avenida Benito Juarez and 90 Avenida Sur, I picked up the aroma of roasted chicken. I'd been walking for about an hour and hadn't yet eaten. I followed the scent to a little hole in the wall setup between a tire shop and a used auto parts store where I discovered two young women turning chickens in a roaster. I smiled and held up my fingers, "Dos, por favor." The girl placed two pieces of chicken into a plastic bag and handed me my side orders -- rice and three kinds of hot sauce, also served in tiny plastic bags. No styrofoam containers, paper plates, or plastic utensils. $40 pesos. I bought a bottle of Pepsi across the street, sat myself down on the curb and dug into the baggies of food with my bare hands. It was one of the most delicious meals I'd eaten since I arrived.

I continued my stroll around the western end of the city -- a neighborhood labeled Ejidal, according to Google Maps -- and looped back to el centro via Avenida Constituyentes, ending at the beach near the end of Avenida Benito Juarez. Everything looking so new and shiny -- new cars, new condos, for sale/for rent signs everywhere -- and yet I couldn't help notice bus load after bus load of indigenous Mexicans -- many of them dressed in hotel attendant white -- riding to jobs that probably paid them less for a day's work than what I make in an hour. I see their dark-skinned faces, solemn and contemplative, staring out those bus windows, staring back at me. The ADO bus terminal is here at the end of Avenida Benito Juarez as is the ferry terminal with ferries leaving for Cozumel every hour or so. After that five-mile walk -- sweaty and hot, sore knees -- it felt so good to dive into the ocean to cool off. It is one of the greatest feelings. I sat on the beach watching tourists lined up on the dock, waiting to board their assigned ship. In the hazy distance, I see the skyscraper hotels along the horizon, like a mirage. For the lucky few, it is a good life.

I took my lunch later that afternoon at a tourist spot along the Fifth Street corridor, a place called Texas BBQ Burger. Yes, I could be a travel snob and shame myself into dining at restaurants that only offer authentic Mexican cuisine. But if I had wanted good Mexican food, I would have just driven into Dallas instead of catching a plane out here to the Yucatan peninsula. Anyway, I was craving a burger. I strike up a conversation with my waiter. He tells me that he rents a room in a condo near Playa del Carmen for $250/month. He pays $2 a month for water and $15 a month for electricity. Originally from Florida, he flies home every six months to reset his visa status. I envy his living/work situation. At some point over the next few years or so, I hope to be doing something very similar -- living a beach bum life while working remotely. 'Digital nomads' is the trendy term people are using these days to describe such a lifestyle. But I have two small dogs, a kid who just started college, and a wife from whom I've been separated for the past few years but haven't yet officially divorced. It's...."complicated."

—

Playa del Carmen - Day 5 - 12/1/16:

Last full day in Mexico. Last day at the beach. The Riviera Maya Jazz Fest 2016 takes place this weekend. I'm sitting next to the stage, toes in the sand, listening to one of the acts do their sound check. I dive into the water and the bass line fades to a distant heartbeat as I dip below the rolling surf. Later, back at home, I learned that I had missed the Steve Gadd Band. Damn. In case you don't know, he's the drummer who played on many of Paul Simon's classic songs, like "50 Ways to Leave Your Lover" and "Late in the Evening."

I love this place. This is Waikiki without the homeless crackheads. Or Ka-anapali without the $100-a-night hotels. This is Cabo San Lucas without the Sammy Hagar Cabo Wabo assholes and back-breaking waves crashing ten-feet high along the shore. This could be Cancun if only they'd stop chasing people from the beaches that front their fancy -- albeit half-empty -- all-inclusive hotels. In fact, I would be returning to Playa Del Carmen seven months later in July 2017 (after another contract gig failed to pan out, but that's another set of trip notes). Everything is so convenient. My hotel is three or four blocks from the beach. Easy walking distance. And between those two points are numerous places to eat, drink, shop.

You don't need to pack a day's worth of food and drink in an ice chest and lug it half a mile over sand and napping beach people; the Oxxo store is right on the corner. (Oxxo stores are convenience stores, similar to 7-Elevens in the States. They can be found everywhere in Yucatan tourist spots.)

I realize tourist mecca and tourist shit hole are two sides of the same coin. I make no claims of being any kind of seasoned travel adventurer. I come here to soak in the Caribbean and decompress. Recharge my batteries before heading back to the grind. Saltwater therapy, I like to call it. I'm willing to put up with a few tourists looking to spend some money for a bit of fun. I'm one of them.

—

Playa del Carmen - Day 6 - 12/2/16 - Going home:
Checked out of my hotel and made my way to the ADO bus station. I noticed a German shepherd frantically sniffing around along Fifth Street. I see him trying to lick the condensation within the bulb of a spot lamp in a flower bed. Next he tries to lick a bit of water from the damp ground. He's panting heavily, and I follow him, trying to keep up with his frantic pace. I stop real quick and buy a liter of bottled water, then run to catch up to him. He's still searching around, panting. Tourists don't seem to notice him. I get near him. He spots me and I show him the bottle of water. I kneel down and pour some water into my cupped hand. He laps it up. I'm crouched there in the middle of Fifth Street with my backpack and shoulder bag. Tourists walking past, oblivious. He looks exhausted and overheated. I dribble some water over his head, then he drinks more from my hand. He sits next to me for a bit before trotting off into the crowd, and I continue my way to the bus station.

The ADO bus station is located at the end of Avenida Benito Juarez where it meets Fifth Street near the beach. Bus tickets to the airport cost $174 pesos and depart every half-hour. Works out to about $9US (at the time of this writing, the price of a ticket has climbed to about $12US). Still cheaper than taking a taxi. Bring a couple of five-pesos coins in order to pay for the restroom. It's one of those unattended setups where you have to drop a coin into the slot and slip through a metal bar turnstile.

At the Cancun airport I see Americans again -- sunburned, boisterous, pear-shaped. They were there on the beach and scattered around town, but it's easier to ignore them in the wild. I am one of them. These are my people. I was merely trying to lose myself. Upon arriving at Fort Lauderdale, the flight attendant says over the PA system: "Welcome to America." He is greeted with laughter. A few people shout "'Merica!" in response. Donald Trump was elected president a week ago, and none of us know exactly how to think or feel about it. It's weird. America is weird. It's as if we'd entered some kind of parallel dimension -- one of an infinite number of possible timelines strung out across the matrix of third-dimensional time and space that should not have occurred.

Trying to catch my flight back to Dallas through Fort Lauderdale was a huge pain in the ass. Getting through immigration at Fort Lauderdale was a huge pain in the ass. Trying to get through customs was one of the most frustrating travel experiences. I nearly missed my connecting flight to Dallas because of all of the bureaucratic, security guard bullshit, very little of which has to do with any kind of real security. It took over an hour to get through customs:

- First, they have you scan your passport and complete the immigration forms at little kiosks.
- Then, you have to wait in another line in order to present your "receipt" of your completed immigration form to a Department of Homeland Security agent.
- Next, you exit and re-enter in order to pass through TSA security before you can proceed to your connecting flight.

If the terrorists really wanted to blow up Florida, they could probably just launch a few missiles from Cuba. Why bear the discomfort of riding in a cramped plane with a bunch of fat Americans?

My connecting flight was originally in Terminal G, the same terminal where my flight from Mexico would be landing, but it was moved to Terminal E on the day of my flight, which was at the opposite end of the airport. I didn't discover this change until I made it past immigration. I ran at a full gallop to make it to the gate and was the very last person to board the plane; the flight attendant shut the plane door as soon as I entered. Sweating and out of breath, I plopped myself down in my seat and smiled at the guy sitting next to me. He looked like a fitness instructor, and his companion -- an older blonde woman who was easily twenty or thirty years his senior -- lay huddled against the window with a sleep shade over her eyes. He smiled calmly at me and opened a book he was reading -- Bill O'Reilly's "Pinheads and Patriots."

Stopped by Vikon Flea Market today to see how things were going. Opening up another used-book shop is always in the back of my mind, but leasing a brick-and-mortar shop is too expensive. I don't see how small businesses can survive. It's as if property developers and city governments are actively working against the small business guys. Outrageous rents, jacked-up utility costs. How can a small business owner hope to turn a profit when the rent for floorspace is $2,500 to $4,000 per month? You've got to make at least double that amount to give you something to take home. Then the city tax assessor comes snooping by and determines how much your business is worth -- the higher the value the more taxes you'll need to pay. You'll get a tax bill at the end of the year. I suppose you can write most of it off come tax time, but why not make it more affordable out the gate?

And so I always find my way back to Vikon Village. It's cheap -- $100 per month for a 10x15 booth. That's how much I was paying when I operated a booth there in 2014. I think now it's gone up to $150. Problem is, they're only open Friday through Sunday. Who knows how long places like this will still be around? I suspect the city sees flea markets as a nuisance business. It's messy, unorganized, the proprietors often eccentric or suffering from some form of mental illness. The owners of Vikon, a Korean family, have already converted half of what used to be flea market space into banquet halls for quinceaneras and other parties, catering mostly to an Hispanic clientele.

—

I poke my head into the Witch Doctor's shop. I hear a woman gabbing behind the partition. His rabbit-eared TV is turned on with the volume turned up and tuned to a channel showing Suze Orman blabbing about financial advice. Sitting on his makeshift "massage" table is Lisa the Dress Lady, an old Chinese woman that maintains a messy dress shop next to my old booth. She's going on and on about problems with her daughter. The Witch Doctor rests his head in his hand, tired like, like he's been listening to her for too long. Lisa tends to go on and on about her problems with her daughter. It's a never-ending drama. Her daughter is fifty years old. Lisa is seventy-two.

But listening to her tell her story, you'd think it was two teen-aged sisters bickering back and forth. The Witch Doctor looks at me and rolls his eyes.

"If I put her in a mental hospital," says Lisa, "she just sit there and smile! Like this!" She smiles while slowly rocking her head from side to side. "See? She crazy! I don't know what to do!"

"You need to get yourself a stick about yay big," says the Witch Doctor, "Then..." He makes a whacking motion.

"You have a lot more books now," I say, inspecting the shelf of books he now has in place of the shelves of rocks and miscellaneous pieces of driftwood that used to be there. The Witch Doctor has been collecting new age and occult books from a friend of his who's been trying to clean out a storage locker. Last time I was here I promised him I'd buy them all, but I've been broke, busy traveling and job-hopping. And anyway, I'd have nowhere to put them except in my own storage locker that I'm renting to store the books for the used-book shop that I've yet to re-open. I try to explain as much, and he just stares at me. "Last week I sold about five hundred bucks worth," he says, which may or may not be true. Next time he might say that he sold a thousand dollars. Or nine hundred. Or two thousand. But his shop is always empty, and it's always just him sitting in the back watching his rabbit-eared TV.

Lisa wants some coffee, and I follow them to the New Age lady's shop. New Age lady is a close friend of the Witch Doctor's. She keeps a pot of Mr. Coffee coffee brewed on a small table amongst the potions, lit candles, and various powders and herbs which supposedly contain magical properties. Tucked away in a little box is a human knee-cap that was carved into the shape of a skull.

I ask the Wiccan Lady if she's familiar with the devic kingdom. She looks puzzled. "Elves, menehunes, faeries," I explain.

She shakes her head. "Well, there are different kinds of Wiccan practices. It's like Christianity and its various denominations. Wiccans usually ask what path are you on? You see? You have to ask what path they're on."

I ask if she has any of Jane Roberts' books. "Who?" she says. I tell her she's the writer of the 'Seth Speaks' series of books.

"Oh, I don't carry any of that stuff."

I've asked her in the past if she had any books by Edgar Cayce or Paul Solomon, and she was equally dismissive. Wiccans seem a lot like Christians in some regards, barely tolerant or aware of concepts which aren't in alignment with their own narrow beliefs.

So I buy a few bundles of white sage instead. We get into a discussion about marijuana legalization, and the Wiccan Lady explains its medicinal qualities. "We used to call it reefer," she says. She elbows the Witch Doctor. "Remember 'Reefer Madness'? That documentary about how bad marijuana was supposed to be?"

—

As we're walking back to the Witch Doctor's shop, he leans toward me. "She goes on and on about marijuana, but she'll never tell you that one of her kids died from a drug overdose."

"Really?"

"She's got another son who's a goddamn pot-head. But she'll never tell you that, either."

Trip Notes: Playa Del Carmen (July 2017)

That gig at Pizza Hut didn't work out. No, not delivering pizzas or making them -- I was hired on to be their lead test automation engineer. My job was to automate the software testing for their in-store point-of-sale systems using a third-party application called eggPlant. But that's neither here nor there. It was just another contract job. Temp work. After seven months of poking around their antiquated system, I decided I'd had enough. I accepted an offer to return to Verizon, a place I'd worked at two years prior.

I often consider writing about my experiences at these companies, but I stop myself -- if they were interesting to read about, maybe I'd still be working there. The work is tedious, the conversations uninteresting. To describe the literal physical aspects of the job is to describe sitting in front of a computer typing on a plastic keyboard. Doesn't matter what you're doing -- software engineer, secretary, manager -- we are all sitting in desk chairs staring at computer screens eight to ten hours a day. The job titles might be different. The pay scales may be off a bit, but it's all basically the same gray world of performing repetitive tasks for the reward of a paycheck every two weeks. It's the same wherever you go. There are no risk-takers working these 9-to-5 gigs. Some people are content being a part of this process. I very rarely felt this way. Nowadays, even less so. But the money is good; the pay tends to be a bit higher in the tech industry. But as you grow older and as the years wear on, you begin to realize that having money no longer seems as important as having time and freedom.

Boredom is the main reason I decide to leave a place.

(Actually, that's a lie.)

Most tech jobs are boring. A lot of people think tech is sexy. Geek is cool, thanks to places like Google or Apple. What people are attracted to is the money. The work itself is often mind-numbingly tedious. You're sitting in an office at a desk in front of a computer eight hours a day. No, I leave because people begin to annoy me to the point where I can barely stand to go into a place. It's not that I don't like them -- the office worker, the cube life workers. I grow weary of the pointless chit-chat, the fakery, and the quiet desperation (as Thoreau once put it). This is no way to spend one's life. Better to leave. Make your money and get the hell out. I've become an expert at quitting jobs -- to paraphrase Robert De Niro's character in 'Heat':

Can you get up and walk away within thirty minutes and leave everything behind? I could list quitting as a skill-set on my resume. "Professional Job-Hopper: Calling it quits in the tech industry for over 25 years." It would make an excellent book title, too. I should write that book.

Putting aside the obvious problem of not having a steady paycheck, quitting a job -- especially a shitty one -- is a liberating feeling. Nothing feels better than submitting your notice of resignation and then not giving a fuck about anything for the next few weeks. The trick is to begin planning your departure your first day on the job. It's like what they teach CIA operatives or security personnel -- when entering a room, be sure to make a mental note of all the exit points. And keep your back to the wall.

—

Before hopping over to that next stop in my job-hopping career, I thought I'd take another trip down to Playa Del Carmen. I had a week to do something, but not a whole lot of money. My original plan was to drive the van down to South Padre Island. After all, that was the reason I bought the thing two years ago – so I could take these kinds of road-trips. But it needed an alignment, and being the middle of summer in Texas, it would be too hot to sleep in, anyway. So I looked into renting a car. A five-day rental would run me about three hundred dollars. I could do that. But I also like to purchase a collision damage waiver insurance policy as well. That brought the total cost up to just over five hundred dollars. So I clicked over to Spirit Airlines and Expedia. Five days in Playa Del Carmen would run me just over six hundred dollars for hotel and plane fare. Five hundred bucks to rent a car to drive down to South Texas? Or six hundred bucks for plane fare and a hotel in Playa Del Carmen? No question about it in my mind. I dumped it all on one of my credit cards. Done.

I was scheduled to fly out three days later that following Sunday.

This trip I had to do on the cheap -- not sleeping in flea-bag hostels without air-conditioning cheap, but cheap enough that I would have enough money to hold me over until my first paycheck when I got to Verizon. Payday wasn't going to be for another month. When I worked at Cisco Systems, nothing beat getting those twelve-thousand-dollar bonuses with three weeks' paid vacation every year, but those days are gone and I'm not interested in going back. I'm nearly fifty years old -- I figure I've got a good ten, twenty years to get out there and see the world. I don't want to become one of those senior citizens you see stuck in rush-hour traffic, forced to remain working stiffs because they're still paying rent or a mortgage or have school-age kids to support. It's a depressing sight -- a tired old, beat-down looking dude hunched over his steering wheel, inching along in traffic and darkness, worn-out face illuminated by the brake lights of the car in front of him -- yet another poor soul whose departure from this world will sometimes be announced on the radio: "Bad news for commuters driving along 635 this morning. A fatality accident has westbound lanes completely shutdown. Traffic is being diverted at Preston Road. Next up....weather on the eights."

—

Doing travel on the cheap means not spending eighty-dollars on a cab ride to the airport when you could spend five bucks riding the train instead, which is why I found myself sitting on a DART train at the Parker Road station at six-thirty in the morning. DART -- Dallas Area Rapid Transit -- is the light-rail system that serves the Dallas Metroplex. If you're from the Bay Area, you're probably familiar with their BART system (Bay Area Rapid Transit). With DART, the actual trains look more like the ones used by San Jose's VTA light-rail system. Quaint, reliable, well-lighted and clean. But slow as hell. It would take me two hours to get from the Parker Road station in Plano to Terminal A at the airport.

Getting from the house to DFW Airport:

$80 cab ride: 20 minutes.

$5 DART rail: 2 hours.

The train departed promptly at 7am, and I arrived at the airport at 8:40am near Terminal A. I had to catch a shuttle bus to take me to Terminal E, and by 9:30am I had made it through the TSA checkpoint and was at the gate. Three hours later I was in the air with Spirit Airlines and headed toward Cancun.

Four hours later, I was waiting outside Cancun International Airport waiting for the ADO bus. Tickets to Playa Del Carmen cost $12US. Again, if I had taken a taxi, it probably would have run me close to $80US. Playa Del Carmen is about an hour away from the airport heading south. Cancun is 30 minutes away heading north. The taxi ride into Cancun's El Centro always runs about $35US.

Getting from Cancun International Airport to Playa Del Carmen:

$80 cab ride: 1 hour (estimate based on previous trips to Cancun).

$12 bus ticket: 1 hour.

Something to be said for doing things on the cheap. Getting to Playa Del Carmen, I was already spending nearly a tenth of what I would have spent if I had gone the expensive route -- $17 total for train ride and bus ticket versus $160 for cab fare. It's slower, but that's okay. I wasn't in any rush -- the beach wasn't going anywhere, and I already had a room reserved at the Hotel Riviera Caribe Maya.

By 5:30pm, I was walking up Fifth Street toward the hotel. My room was situated in a peculiar spot away from the rest of the hotel. You had to walk through the pool area -- being mindful not to slip and fall in as you negotiated a narrow path -- and up a flight of rickety wooden stairs to get to it. A wooden deck overlooking part of the hotel roof led to the entrance of my room, which was a sliding-glass patio door. My hotel key appeared to have been fashioned from an old drill-bit, and to lock or unlock the patio door I had to insert this "key" into a hole that had been drilled into the door just beneath the handle. It all looked sort of home-made, and I was a little disturbed by it. Inside, a frosted glass shower door led to the bathroom. If you tried to swing it open all the way it would bump against the nightstand sitting next to the bed. Another sliding door revealed a closet with wooden shelving. In one corner of the room, resting upon a makeshift wooden triangular cabinet, upon which I would use my laptop computer, was a tiny 14-inch flat-screen TV. It was unplugged and remained that way the duration of my visit. It was a strange setup, this room, but I grew accustomed to it after a while, and since it was situated away from all the other rooms, I was able to enjoy a little more privacy and didn't have to worry about other guests walking by my door.

—

A thunderstorm kicked up as I was about to head out to find something to eat. I tried to wait it out but grew impatient. I hadn't eaten anything since that stale bagel and bottle of orange juice at the airport in Dallas twelve hours earlier (which cost $6US, by the way -- what a ripoff). Somewhere between there and here I developed a painful sinus headache. It felt like a steel-toed combat boot inside my head trying to kick its way out.

Off I went sloshing through puddles in my flip-flops and trying to find a place with indoor dining. Mini flash-floods poured through the streets and pooled in areas where storm drains were overflowing and clogged. I ducked into a place that looked to have a lot of available seating -- La Parilla, a touristy Tex-Mex place that most times I probably would have avoided, and in this case I probably should have. The chicken enchiladas were bland. The tortillas were stale. The cheese tasted as if it had been frozen and reheated. I don't recall how much I paid, but it was too much for this garbage. Walking back to the hotel trying to avoid the puddles and streams of what I assumed was raw sewage, I tried to recount the crappy places I had eaten at during my travels, which always seemed to occur within the first night upon arriving in a city for the first time -- you're hungry, you're tired, you don't know where to go -- you pick the first place you find without giving it much thought. I ignore travel guides or travel blogs on the Internet when it comes to finding places to eat. Restaurants change too much -- new owners, new management, high turnover rate with the cooks and wait staff. You gotta sniff 'em out, try 'em out. Any review older than a few months is meaningless. And for this trip I had just broken the primary rule -- which was doing things on the cheap. Eating at touristy shit-holes is not doing things on the cheap.

The next morning I awoke with that same combat boot in the head migraine. The previous night's dinner and those three bottles of Mexican beer were of little help. Being in the Caribbean, I knew just the cure -- I headed for the beach and jumped into the water. I did a few underwater hand-stands and curled myself up into a ball and twirled myself forwards and backwards underwater a few times. The saltwater eventually flushed out whatever was clogging my sinuses. The pressure in my head slowly dissipated, and I began to feel normal again. Both nostrils completely clear, breathing free and easy -- all done without the aid of man-made pharmaceuticals.

Later, I walked to the Mega store along Avenida Constituyentes. Mega stores are large grocery stores in Mexico that come complete with a deli and bakery. You can usually spot them a few blocks away by their large signs that say "MEGA" with a logo of a pelican next to it. I picked up a package of salami, some gouda cheese, and a bag of freshly-baked croissants. This would serve as my breakfast and lunch for the next few days. Total cost was less than $10US. Half way back to the hotel, I couldn't wait -- I sat down on the sidewalk and had a meal right there on the spot, ripping open that package of salami and digging into that gouda cheese with my stainless steel survival spork. I miss the days when you were allowed to pack a pocket knife in your carry-on luggage. Having something a little sharper than a glorified spoon would have made cutting into that cheese a lot less messy.

—

153

I really only had three full days to lounge around at the beach. Three days is a decent amount of soak time. Spending more time beyond that in the same spot would become tedious. If I had more time I would have taken a day trip up to Cancun and caught the ferry to Isla Mujeres, but I'd been there so many times, during happier times with the wife and kid, that it would begin to seem too much like rehashing old memories. And anyway, I was there just six months ago. I have little interest in revisiting Memory Lane. There are too many new streets to discover and explore. Or maybe I would have caught the ferry to Cozumel, a place I'd never visited but by all accounts looked pretty much the same as my spot along the beach in Playa Del Carmen. So why bother?

Three days is hardly enough time to go adventuring and exploring. It's taken me ten years to really get a feel for my own home town in north Dallas and its surrounding neighborhoods. I hesitate to say DFW since I've rarely ventured to the "FW" part -- Fort Worth. I've been content with spending most of my time around Dallas.

Three days isn't so much a vacation as it is a quick decompression -- a way to blast out of the atmosphere to enjoy the weightlessness of time and space for a brief moment, to luxuriate in the temporary illusion of having no responsibilities or obligations -- a quick recalibration so you can come back and hit the ground running at a higher frequency. Or hope to. Once again my thoughts drifted to pondering how I could live this sort of life, this beach bum life, for the rest of my life. It seems so easy when your hotel reservation has already been paid and that return ticket has already been booked. But reality begins to creep in as your bank account approaches zero, and suddenly returning home to be that working stiff stuck in rush-hour traffic doesn't seem like such a bad idea.

—

Beach, eat, sleep. There are no epiphanies or flashes of inspiration. Touchy-feely artsy sensitivity has given way to a kind of vague, reptilian awareness. I awake in the morning, walk to the Oxxo store across the street for my daily cup of coffee. Return to the hotel, take a shit, brush my teeth. Then head to the water for a quick dip while the beach is still empty. At this hour of the morning, the hordes of tourists are still asleep in their hotels; there are only a few joggers out and perhaps a senior citizen or two staggering along the uneven sand. I have the place to myself. I sit and think and play with the sand between my fingers and toes and pretend that each grain is a universe unto its own crumbling and cascading into an infinite number of other universes. How many atoms in a grain of sand? How many universes in each atom? I bask in the orange glow of the morning sun as it begins its ascent above the horizon.

Except for the waiters who take my order at restaurants along Fifth Street, I speak to very few people. This is usually the case when I travel. Even while I vacationed with the wife and kid, I often ventured out alone to walk around and soak in the experiences of my new environment. going for hour-long jaunts around town, depending on the heat, usually in the morning with my large cup of Oxxo coffee. Travel for me has never been a social affair. Making new friends and meeting new people have never been a part of my itinerary. If it happens, fine. If not, it doesn't matter. Perhaps due to my tendency toward being an antisocial loner or because I feel intimidated by large crowds of people having fun and enjoying themselves -- whatever the reason, I've tended to experience new cultures quietly and from a distance.

Full cultural immersion isn't possible when you're only visiting a place for two to three weeks. Always fleeting, always temporary -- but I absorb what I can. Some would argue there is very little culture to find in tourist trap places like Cancun or Playa Del Carmen. I say it's naive to visit these places and expect the locals to be living just as they did a hundred or a thousand years ago. Do people visit Boston and expect the locals to be wearing pilgrim outfits? Life is now, and people want new things. They want to enjoy the benefits of technological advancements. They want Internet access and cell phones with unlimited voice and text. And if the locals happen to be living in a beautiful spot of the world, obviously foreigners will want to visit and have a look around. This is human nature. This is the human journey. Life itself, our spiritual journey, is a kind of tour through this plane of existence. Enjoy it while you can. All of it.

The last time I left Playa Del Carmen, I made the mistake of buying my ADO bus ticket a day in advance. I thought I was being smart. I showed up the next morning two hours before my bus was scheduled to depart and watched as bus after bus bound for the airport came and went. Buses depart for the airport every thirty minutes. I couldn't board an earlier bus since my ticket was for the one scheduled to depart at 12:30pm. Reserved seating is strictly enforced. Planning, scheduling, logistics -- it all makes sense on paper and conceptually, but sometimes it takes reality to point out the obvious errors in one's thinking. And I probably shouldn't have arrived two hours early, either.

The second time around I knew better than to be too anal about it. I showed up when I showed up and bought a ticket for the next bus to the airport, which was now. Within fifteen minutes I was on my way back to Cancun International.

ADO buses aren't filthy and grungy like Greyhound buses back in the States. They're clean, comfortable, and the buses I caught were always on time. You actually have room to stretch out your legs. The air-conditioning blows so cold that many people bring sweaters to wear during the journey. These buses are made for comfort and enjoyment, unlike Greyhound where you are treated to the depressing experience of knowing what it's like to ride an inner-city bus on your way to prison. Not so with ADO -- you're on vacation traveling down the Caribbean coastline. Lean back, enjoy the ride. Champagne wishes and caviar dreams.

After getting through customs, I caught the shuttle to Terminal A, walked to the DART rail station and caught the rush-hour train to Parker Road station back in good ol' Plano, Texas. As the train snaked its way through the Irving tech corridor and into downtown Dallas, it became more and more crowded with commuters making their way home after a long day on the job. Faces looking worn, beat down, tired. I felt as if I had some great secret to tell everyone. You don't have to keep doing this, people! You don't have to work like slaves! Go ahead, tell your boss to fuck off, take a vacation, run up your credit card debt! It doesn't matter! The illusion is one of your own creation!

But no one likes to hear from the guy who just got back from vacation, so I kept quiet, heading home toward a familiar yet uncertain future.

Made in United States
Orlando, FL
24 May 2024

47166640R00088